THREE GREEN BOTTLES

DOMINIC DEVINE

three green bottles

PUBLISHED FOR THE CRIME CLUB BY
DOUBLEDAY & COMPANY, INC.
GARDEN CITY, NEW YORK, 1972

6837

All of the characters in this book
are fictitious, and any resemblance
to actual persons, living or dead,
is purely coincidental.

ISBN: 0-385-00121-5
Library of Congress Catalog Card Number 72-76150
Copyright © 1972 by Dominic Devine
All Rights Reserved
Printed in the United States of America
First Edition in the United States of America

PROLOGUE TO PART I

Janice Allen finished her history essay in a petulant scrawl. It wasn't up to standard, she could already see the reproof "Unworthy of you" appended in red pencil in Mr. Baines's neat script. A bit of a creep, that man, even if he did make such a fuss of her. He had the oddest way of looking at her.

Anyway, he shouldn't be setting homework just two weeks from the summer holidays. And the hottest July for seventeen years, it said on T.V. last night.

It was half-past six. Janice dashed upstairs, stripped off, stepped into her yellow bathing suit, and put shorts and a T shirt on top. Gathering a bathing towel, she went down to the kitchen to rummage for food.

Her mother was making a salad.

"Daddy not home yet?" Janice asked as she opened the fridge door. She took out a couple of tomatoes.

"No, he's still at the shop. He won't be back till after seven."

Blast! She'd have to walk, then, for her bike had a puncture. She'd been hoping for a lift from her father.

She cut two slices of bread and began to spread them.

"Go easy on that butter!" her mother said. "You'd think we didn't feed you. If you'd eat properly at *mealtimes* . . ."

Janice let the voice drone on. Silence was the most effective answer when grown-ups were being tiresome.

When her mother paused for breath, she said: "Are there no Cokes left?"

"You ought to know."

She did know. "Well, can I have some of next week's pocket money? I'll be *dehydrated* if I've nothing to drink." She'd learned that word yesterday in school from Miss Carey.

Her mother sighed, took her purse from a shopping bag and handed Janice some change. "Where are you going?"

Janice was wrapping her sandwiches. "Abbot's Creek," she said. "Who with?"

"The usual gang."

"Well, be careful. Remember you're not as strong a swimmer as the others."

The same sermon every night. And Janice knew what would come next: don't be late.

"And don't be late," her mother said.

"No, Mummy. But I'll have to *walk*, remember!"

Now at last she was outside, and felt the sun's heat beating on her face. Gosh, this was awful! How was she going to walk all that distance to the creek?

She crossed to Napoli's and bought a Coke. If she had to drink it on the way (she was thirsty already), maybe one of the others would take pity and share hers. Not Lesley—she'd let her dehydrate first. But Anne, maybe, or Pat.

When she came out of Napoli's a car had pulled up just down the road and the driver was putting a letter in the postbox. Janice recognised her. "Hello, Miss Carey," she called.

The woman turned round. "Oh, it's Janice! Going swimming?"

"Yes."

"Where?"

"Abbot's Creek."

"Good gracious! That's a long way."

"Yes, Miss Carey." Janice achieved exactly the right note of brave resignation.

"Hop in. I'll take you."

"Oh, I couldn't—"

"Don't be silly. It's partly on my way."

Janice needed no further persuasion.

It was a green 1968 Mini, its paintwork gleaming, and the interior clean and tidy. So different from her father's ancient Lanchester, which was held together by string and had everything but the kitchen sink piled on the back seat.

Miss Carey was popular at school, everybody was mad about

her. And super to look at, too—great big eyes, and long, glossy black hair, and that funny little scar on her cheek.

She was engaged, or as good as, to Dr. Kendall, who lived with the Armitages. Some of the girls at school said that Mr. Baines nursed a secret passion for her. But Janice was sure that wasn't true.

Miss Carey said: "It's nearly hot enough to tempt *me* in."

"Oh, I wish you would!" Janice tried to inject enthusiasm into her voice.

Shelagh Carey laughed. "Don't worry, I'm not serious . . . Anyway, I've a cold. I'm going home to bed."

As they neared the creek, Miss Carey overtook three cyclists: it was Lesley, Anne and Pat.

Janice waved, but wasn't sure if they'd recognised her. "This will do fine, thank you, Miss Carey," she said.

The car pulled up by the stile which led onto the golf course on the left. Twenty yards further on was the path leading down to Abbot's Creek.

Janice got out and made a performance of thanking Miss Carey. The cyclists were near enough to recognise her now, *and* the driver. This would put Lesley's nose out of joint for a week: she imagined she had some special relationship with Miss Carey.

The car drove off, and the four girls made their way down to the sandy beach. Janice felt smug when she saw how hot and dusty the others looked as they wheeled their bikes.

There were two girls already on the beach. One was on her back on the sand while the other straddled her and pinned her arms down.

"Let me up, Celia, you're *hurting* me," the girl underneath wailed.

"Well, say it, then. Go on, *say* it: 'I'm a bastard!' I'll let you go, I promise."

Janice stepped forward. "You'll let her go anyway," she said. Sometimes she was scared of Celia Armitage. But tonight, with her friends on hand, she could afford to show off a little.

Celia whipped her head round. "Oh, it's *you*," she said viciously. "Keep out of this!"

But her attention had been sufficiently distracted. Her prisoner gave a sudden heave and wriggle and was up and away. It was Helen Potts, Janice noted: she *was* a bastard, too.

Celia made no attempt to follow. She stood glaring at Janice. "Someday I'll kill you," she said. "I'll kill the lot of you."

Janice said: "Grow up," turned on her heel and joined her friends, who were already undressing, taking no part in the exchange.

It was creepy, Janice thought, the way Celia had said that: "I'll kill the lot of you." She had a screw loose, everybody knew that. Suppose she went *berserk* one day . . .

Although the same age as herself—thirteen—Celia was still in the junior school with the eleven-year-olds. She really ought to be in a home, it wasn't safe the way she carried on.

By the time Janice was ready, the other three were in the water, and Lesley was showing off as usual, diving from that big rock, then swimming away out with the lazy crawl which looked so effortless but which Janice couldn't match.

Lesley's prowess almost spoiled Janice's pleasure in swimming. They were rivals in the classroom, always first and second, or first equal. Well, except in subjects like maths and science, where Anne Ridley had the field to herself.

No one could be jealous of Anne, who was so even-tempered and couldn't care less what others thought of her. But Lesley was a *swot*, she wasn't really clever, she just worked like stink and sucked up to the teachers. Privately Janice resolved to rewrite that history essay when she got home; she wasn't going to have Lesley beating her in that.

The sea was super tonight, like a warm bath. She soon forgot her irritation. Anyway, her crawl was definitely improving—Anne said so when she asked her. And Anne was an even better swimmer than Lesley.

It was after nine before they came out of the water. The air was still warm enough for them to sit in their wet costumes while they ate their picnic. In fact, Anne rolled her costume right down and sat topless. Janice was secretly a little shocked, even though by now the beach was deserted.

They were still sunbathing when a woman came down the path from the road and crossed the sands to where they sat. It was Celia's mother.

"You haven't seen Celia, have you?" she asked.

Lesley said: "She was here ages ago, Mrs. Armitage. But she went away."

"You don't know where?"

They shook their heads.

Mrs. Armitage was glancing at Anne, who hadn't bothered to pull up her costume. It was impossible to embarrass Anne.

Finally Mrs. Armitage said: "Are these your bicycles up there?"

"Yes," Anne said. They'd left them up near the bank.

"I only saw *three*. You'd better check—"

"No, it's all right, Jan hasn't got hers—she's walking home."

Mrs. Armitage nodded. "Well, if Celia comes back, tell her she's to go straight home." She sounded anxious.

Janice yawned. She hadn't meant to be rude: the yawn just came and she couldn't stop it.

Mrs. Armitage said sharply: "I don't know why you're all so unfriendly to Celia. You especially, Janice. She *likes* you."

"Well, she has a funny way of showing it," Janice said. But that *was* rude. "I'm sorry, Mrs. Armitage, I didn't mean that."

"She doesn't keep well, you know."

Janice yawned again. Gosh, this was *terrible!* It must be the sun, or something.

It was too much for Mrs. Armitage, who turned abruptly and walked away.

Pat Richards said: "You shouldn't have done that, Jan."

Janice flushed. "I didn't mean to," she said.

They discussed the Armitages. They all agreed that Dr. Armitage was a harmless old stick and that his wife wore the trousers.

"She's too possessive," Janice said. She felt she had to justify her rudeness by criticising Mrs. Armitage. "Fancy coming out at nine o'clock to search for your thirteen-year-old daughter!"

"Half-past nine," Pat—a stickler for accuracy—amended.

"Well, half-past, then. She's *ruined* her family. Look at Mandy!"

Mandy was the stepsister, very prim and remote. An odd-looking girl with glasses and a pony-tail.

Lesley said: "There's nothing wrong with Mandy. She's *nice*."

"Just because she's your Sunday-school teacher."

"Don't be silly! I know her because she used to go with Kenny."

But it was too hot to quarrel. "Has anyone any Coke left?" Janice said. "I'm *dehydrated*."

No one had. Lesley suggested another swim before they got dressed.

Anne said: "I dare you to go in starkers."

She had no takers. But she herself stepped out of her costume and walked unhurriedly down to the water, not even looking round to make sure there was no one watching.

Janice was really shocked this time. No one'll ever see *me* like that, she thought. Anne was too precocious, that was her trouble, she was copying her older sister. She even waggled her bottom the same way. Disgusting!

When they came out of the water this time, the sun had dipped below the horizon and there was a nip in the air. Janice's teeth were chattering by the time she was dried and dressed. And she was very conscious of how late it was. She decided she would take the short cut home across the golf course.

The other three got their own back as they wheeled their bicycles up to the road. "Where's Miss Carey?" Lesley said. "Didn't you ask her to call back?"

And Pat said: "Gosh, rather you than me, Jan! Nearly a mile, and all uphill!"

"It's much shorter by the golf course," Janice said.

"You're not going *that* way, surely? It's getting dark." Pat was a timid creature.

They got on their bikes. "Good hiking, Jan," one of them said, and they all laughed. Then they were gone.

Janice stood looking after them, vaguely resentful. There was no call for them to *laugh,* it wasn't funny. She had spent too long practising the crawl tonight, and her arms and legs were aching. She was cold.

A car passed, going towards the town. Why not hitch a lift, she thought? Her parents need never know.

She sat on the grass verge and waited. She'd give it five minutes, she decided. If she hadn't got a lift by then, she'd climb over the stile and walk across the golf course.

Everyone said she was born lucky; things fell into her lap. Look how Miss Carey had appeared like the fairy godmother tonight just when she was needed.

Someone would come along.

Someone did.

PART I

MANDY ARMITAGE

CHAPTER I

On the night Janice Allen disappeared, I was sunbathing in the garden after supper. About half-past nine Terry Kendall came across the lawn from the house and—

No, that's too abrupt. Who is Terry Kendall? Who am I? I have to start at the beginning.

I knew them all, you see. I knew Janice, Terry, Shelagh, all the characters in the drama that played itself out in Chalford last year. I was, you might say, the link, the common element. So who am I?

They christened me Amanda because my mother had been to *Private Lives* and the name appealed to her. But from the start I was Mandy.

I never saw my mother, for she died the day after I was born. Until I was six, her mother and father brought me up at their farm in Dorset. Daddy used to visit me two or three times a year; and I always spent a month in the summer at Chalford under the stern eye of his housekeeper. Daddy himself I rarely saw: he was a doctor and always busy. Or else his asthma was bad.

Looking back now, and making due allowance for memory's rose-tinted spectacles, I think those six years were happy years. I loved my grandparents, and they were fond of me.

Then my father married again. I was whisked up north for the wedding and I met this elegant stranger who told me I'd be coming to live with her in Chalford and I must learn to call her "Mummy."

I never did learn that. We compromised eventually on "Aunt Gwen"; in recent years I've dropped the "Aunt."

Let me be fair to Gwen: she did try. At least I think she did. She always claimed I was the one who wouldn't cooperate, and I expect she was right. But I was only six, after all, and I missed my grandparents.

When he married Gwen, Daddy bought a much bigger house on Tramore Avenue. His practice must have been doing well, because in those days the avenue was even more exclusive than it is now.

They led quite a gay life to begin with. They entertained a lot and there always seemed to be people around. Daddy used to grumble that he couldn't get his feet up by his own fireside of an evening. But I don't think he minded really.

I was seven and a half when Celia was born. She was a puny child, often ailing, but her mother doted on her. For a while Gwen was one of a group of young mothers who regularly met in each other's houses to drool over their offspring.

But these exchanges tailed off when Celia was slower than the other children to develop. She was nearly three before she walked, and at four she still hadn't more than a few basic words.

That was what provoked the first rift in the marriage. Daddy could see the child wasn't normal; and said so. Gwen was furious: neither then nor later would she ever admit that Celia was mentally backward. It was all physical—the result of inheriting her father's asthma.

Although the quarrel was patched up, things were never quite the same again. And it was soon after this that Uncle Ben—Dr. Radford—joined the practice as Daddy's assistant. He wasn't really an uncle, of course, but he stayed in our house for several years, and Celia and I have always called him Uncle Ben.

It's difficult now at the age of twenty to look back and see events through the eyes of an eleven-year-old girl. At the time the reasons for what happened were obscure in the way grown-up motivations often were. Only gradually over the years was I able to piece together a coherent story.

From the start Uncle Ben made a fuss over Celia. I've no great opinion of him as a doctor: he relies too much on hunches and on antibiotics. But he's conscientious. And he has a way with children.

He showed endless patience in treating Celia's asthma and her hay fever and her allergies (I have the allergies but I've been spared the other two). It was the way to Gwen's heart.

At some point they became lovers. I've no direct proof, merely what you might call circumstantial evidence. No other explanation fits the facts.

Uncle Ben would be about twenty-six then, and very handsome; he's not bad even yet. Gwen was in her early thirties, but looked younger. She really was terrific in those days—it's only in the last year or two the bloom has faded.

No, considering it dispassionately, I can see it was a natural, almost inevitable, consequence of their living in the same house.

One night I was wakened by a crash from downstairs, and as I sat up I heard Daddy and Gwen shouting at each other. It went on and on. I crept down and listened outside the sitting-room door.

Some of it I couldn't hear, a great deal I couldn't understand. But I do remember Gwen saying (this was after the shouting had stopped and they were talking in flat, spent voices): "Well, it's like this, John. If he goes, I'll leave you."

"I can't keep him on in the practice after this." I realised they were talking about Uncle Ben.

"That's up to you. But don't say you haven't been warned."

"What about the children?" Even through the closed door I could detect his wheezing. He always had an attack when he was excited or angry.

"I'll take Celia with me," Gwen said. "You're welcome to Mandy."

At that point I went back upstairs.

A few days later Uncle Ben took a flat in town. Gwen moved into another bedroom. The significance of the changes escaped me: at eleven I was unusually innocent.

Uncle Ben still paid professional visits to Celia, but always at times when Daddy was at home. He was made a partner soon after—it may have been part of the bargain. For years he never visited us socially. The embargo was finally lifted for a birthday party of Celia's; and after that he was made welcome. I suppose Daddy felt the danger was past.

After Uncle Ben moved out, Gwen became even more possessive over Celia. My stepsister was a destructive child and knew how to bait me: my books, my big teddy bear, my clothes, my person—all were fair game. And when appealed to, Gwen invariably took Celia's part.

Daddy saw what was going on, but never intervened. He was a coward, and lazy into the bargain. It's a terrible thing, but I despise my father and I hate my stepmother.

Not that I hated her at that stage. Not consciously, anyway. I was hurt and resentful; much in need of love and not finding it anywhere. At school I had few friends and no close ones. I was too reticent. Not shy, really, just reluctant to confide in others in case they laughed at me.

Until the age of fourteen I was a small child. Then suddenly I shot up and acquired curves in the right places. I remember one night looking at myself in a mirror after my bath and thinking: I'm not going to be ugly after all! I was beginning to look like that picture of my mother I kept in a drawer in my bedroom.

I began to revise my ideas of the spinster life I'd thought I was heading for. Boys were showing an interest; and in due course came invitations—to a cafe, to a film, to the school dance. Invitations which I refused, because I was scared of boys and because of Gwen's attitude.

"You're far too young to be thinking about boys," Gwen used to say. She did her best to discourage them: my clothes were always an inch or two too long (it was in the days of the mini) and my hair too short.

So I drifted on till I was seventeen and in my last year at school, at once fascinated and repelled by boys, and totally without experience. And then came Kenny Peterson.

Of course, he'd been there all along, he'd been in my year since we started secondary school. But I'd never really noticed him until that day my bike skidded and I fell off, scattering my school books into the gutter.

Kenny, who was passing, helped me retrieve them. I had skinned my knee and was nearly in tears. He insisted on taking me into the Bonaventure for a coffee.

That's how it began. It's easy to make fun of adolescent love. But I don't believe anything in life can ever be quite so perfect. We lived for each other, thought about each other all the time. And talked. How wonderful it was to have someone I could unburden myself to, all reserve gone. It was a new world to me, a *shared* world.

Knowing Gwen's views, I said nothing at home about Kenny. They must have wondered why I was out so much in the evenings. But it was summer and they could hardly object, seeing that Daddy was always lecturing me about not getting enough fresh air.

When Kenny took me to his home, his parents were friendly, though I thought his mother looked a bit uneasy. His two younger sisters, Karen and Lesley, teased him all the time.

For six weeks the idyll continued. The happiest weeks of my life: beyond any comparison the happiest.

Then Celia let the cat out of the bag. It was surprising she hadn't found out sooner: she was a malicious child who delighted to carry tales.

On the surface Gwen was very reasonable about it. "Why didn't you tell us, Mandy? You must bring him home to meet us." So I did.

Kenny was nervous, which didn't help; but even at his best he couldn't have coped with Gwen, who played the lady of the manor graciously entertaining an uncouth tenant. She got him to say (though I'm sure she knew already) that his father was an electrician in the shipyard and that his mother worked in a shop. Poor Kenny, who had never been ashamed of his parents before, was made to feel ashamed. And all the time Daddy sat there, pipe in mouth, hardly saying a word. I went cold inside from humiliation and anger. That's when I started to hate my stepmother.

It made no difference, Kenny and I vowed afterwards. But it did. I could feel the change of atmosphere next time I was in his house: I was no longer made to feel welcome. Kenny must have told them of his reception at Tramore Avenue.

Soon he started making excuses for not seeing me. And eventually he suggested we should break it off for a trial period. We were very young, weren't we? And he still had his university degree to work for. Of course, he still *loved* me, but . . .

"Thanks, Kenny," I said. "It's been fun knowing you." And walked away. Just like that.

I didn't see Kenny for years, though I heard of him from time to time through his younger sister, Lesley. Not that I was interested: the part of me that had loved Kenny Peterson was dead.

Once bitten, twice shy. I took protective measures for the future: I made my appearance as unattractive as I could, bought those rimless spectacles that—later—Terry Kendall objected to, scraped my hair back in a pony-tail, welcomed the drab clothes my step-mother liked me to wear.

And I took to religion. Well, I'd been brought up to go to church regularly, but now it became a conscious choice rather than habit. I volunteered to teach in Sunday school. I was secretary of the Youth Association for a while. And eventually I became interested in spastic children; for the past two years I've been doing voluntary work in the Marchmont Hospital for spastics in my spare time.

I dare say there's something Freudian in all this. Other girls who've been ditched get over it and don't go rushing off to a nunnery, so to speak. Well, I couldn't help that: it's how I'm made. For a long time I couldn't understand my stepmother's motive in driving a wedge between Kenny and me. It wasn't until Terry Kendall . . . But that's anticipating.

On leaving school, I took a secretarial course at the local commercial college. I'd have done better to cut loose, leave Chalford, start a new life elsewhere. But I was too timid, I'd lost my new-found confidence. Better, it seemed, the evil I knew than the evil I didn't.

And for the same reason, after I'd qualified, I accepted Daddy's offer to take me on as secretary/receptionist. I'm sure any psychiatrist or family counsellor would have advised against it. But I didn't consult anyone.

Before me there had only been a part-time secretary—a not very efficient married woman. There was much to be done. The practice had expanded rapidly since Dr. Cohen—the ablest of the three partners—joined it a year or two back. There was talk already of engaging an assistant.

I organised a proper appointments system, typed and filed their correspondence and generally made life smoother for them. Daddy was impressed. I don't think he'd expected too much from his cranky elder daughter.

I'd been working in the office about a year when Terry Kendall was taken on as assistant and came to live with us on Tramore Avenue. He was really groovy and looked far too young to be a qualified doctor.

Gwen was captivated by him. He flattered her outrageously, deferred to her opinions, listened patiently to her daily bulletin on Celia's health. I was nauseated.

His attitude to me both at home and in the surgery was for some time correct and formal. But one morning when I'd made his coffee and was leaving the office, he stopped me.

"Don't go," he said. "Have a cup with me."

"I've too much to do—"

"What are you scared of, Mandy? I don't bite."

He stretched forward and whipped off my glasses.

I gasped.

"No, just a minute," he said and walked round behind me. In seconds he had untied the ribbon on the pony-tail and was shaking out my hair.

"Just as I thought," he murmured. "Beautiful, beautiful."

I found my voice. "Will there be anything else, Dr. Kendall?"

"Plenty," he said. "I'd like to see some make-up on your face. And I'd like to take you round the boutiques. You've a super figure, why not wear clothes that do it justice? Why should a rose so fair be born to blush unseen?" He was making theatrical gestures with his arms.

I smiled. It was impossible to be angry with him. And at the sixth time of asking I agreed to have a date with him. Just for once. Just to stop him badgering me.

We had dinner in Moorend one night after my stint at the hospital. Before we went into the hotel Terry insisted on untying my pony-tail and removing my glasses. He quoted Dorothy Parker: "Men seldom make passes at girls who wear glasses."

"I don't want men to make passes," I objected.

"Nonsense! Every girl does. And every girl should let her hair down occasionally."

From the start I was able to relax with Terry, to drop my guard, as I couldn't with anyone else. He had a child-like innocence, and despite all that happened later, that's the quality that for me he still represents: innocence.

When he asked me out again the following week, I accepted. Soon we were having dates once or twice a week. After three months he proposed to me.

But by then I had learned a great deal more about Terry Kendall.

CHAPTER 2

Terry was the elder son of Godfrey Kendall, consultant orthopaedic surgeon in one of the big London hospitals. An uncle was Vice-Chancellor of a university in Canada. Much was expected of Terry. Too much, as it turned out.

He'd inherited the brains, not the character: he lacked application, was easily led astray, easily discouraged. After doing well enough at school, he was persuaded by his father to read medicine —a mistake, this, for his heart was never in it.

In his second year at Barts he got into bad company and from then on floundered from one crisis to another. If it wasn't debts, it was a girl, and if it wasn't a girl, it was university discipline. His father bailed him out of several jams.

Eventually Terry scraped through his finals. But in his first hospital appointment he was in hot water again. There was an incident involving a nurse which almost earned him the sack. He was blameless, he assured me, it was all a misunderstanding.

Misunderstanding or not, it was the last straw for his father, who washed his hands of the black sheep of the family. (Mark, the younger brother, was already showing the qualities he had looked for in vain in Terry.)

A month later his father died of a coronary. Although his death was quite unconnected, Terry didn't see it like that. He had a breakdown and was off work for months. When eventually he completed his internship, he did a series of locums up and down the country. His appointment as assistant to my father and his partners was his first semi-permanent post.

He heard of the vacancy through Tom Baines, a friend of his undergraduate days now teaching in Chalford. Baines knew Uncle Ben and put in a word for Terry. But it was probably his father's name which got him the job; they couldn't have known his whole record.

Terry tried hard to redeem himself. The trouble was, he had a skin that was paper-thin. The least thing could plunge him into the depths: criticism of his work from my father, a letter from his brother, a thoughtless word from me. His ready smile was often a cloak to conceal unhappiness.

I didn't like the sound of that brother. He too had gone in for medicine, but he'd come out top of his year and was now on a post-graduate fellowship in Boston. The letters he wrote Terry were tactless and smug. Yet Terry had an enormous regard for him and took every word to heart. When eventually I met Mark—but that's anticipating again.

Meanwhile my friendship with Terry blossomed. The second or third time out I let him kiss me, and his appetite grew fast after that. But I gave him clear notice of my limits and after some sulking he accepted them. To be honest, it wasn't so much moral scruples on my part as fear of the unknown. I play safe by instinct —it's why I'm such a dull person.

Anyway I wasn't in love with Terry. I liked him a lot, but I didn't love him, he wasn't another Kenny Peterson.

Terry got his sex elsewhere, using our Labrador as an excuse to go out in the late evening. When I taxed him with it, he admitted he was seeing a girl from the new town. Meg, he called her; I never heard her surname. They usually met on the golf course.

She had somehow acquired a key to a workshed near the ninth green—the green which was later to be pictured in every newspaper in the country. But there I go, jumping ahead again. . . .

"Meg means nothing to me," Terry said. I realised he needed sex as a diabetic needs insulin.

I wasn't upset over Meg. On the contrary, she eased my conscience about refusing to sleep with Terry.

That same evening he proposed to me, partly, I suspect, in relief at the way I'd taken the news of Meg. He may even have imagined he was in love with me.

He'd had lots of girls in his time, but I guess I was different. More prudish but also, perhaps, more understanding. I saw behind the smile, I recognised how vulnerable he was, how easily hurt. My role was to bolster his ego, to lift him out of his depressions.

So perhaps he mistook gratitude for love. Anyway he asked me to marry him. I said no. And we went on as before.

The main consulting rooms were in a concrete extension at the back of our house on Tramore Avenue. But the practice also rented a room in Vine Street in the new housing area, where we provided a nightly surgery, Health Service patients only. Daddy was never on duty in Vine Street: he claimed that the fumes from the neighbouring tannery affected his asthma. The other three doctors shared a weekly rota.

When Terry was consulting in Vine Street, I sometimes, if I was free, drove out there and waited for him in the Greyhound across the road.

It was in that pub I met Tom Baines. He came in one night just as Terry and I were leaving. Terry introduced us, and we all sat down and had a drink.

Baines was in his late twenties—a year or two older than Terry. Lean and handsome if you liked that kind of face. I didn't: the carefully tended moustache put me off for a start.

After a degree in history at Cambridge, he had read for the Bar. That was when he got to know Terry.

Mark Kendall claimed it was Tom who first led Terry from the paths of virtue. My own belief was they interacted on each other. At any rate Tom failed the Bar examinations and had to be content with schoolteaching.

He now looked and sounded like a man soured by failure. There was a discontented droop to his mouth, and he spoke in a sarcastic drawl.

Uncle Ben had mentioned Tom occasionally; they went fishing together. I'd seen this man around Chalford, but never connected the name to the face.

He said: "So you're the reason I've been seeing so little of Terry." His tone was not friendly. "I know your sister," he added.

"Celia?"

"Yes. We have her at school. She's pretty dim."

Terry said: "Mandy's only a *half*-sister."

But I preferred my own defensive tactics of silence.

The pair of them began talking about me as if I weren't there.

"I don't see a ring on her finger," said Tom.

"She turned me down."

Baines laughed. "Sensible girl. I could tell her a thing or two about you that would make her hair curl. . . ."

Afterwards I said to Terry: "I *loathe* that man."

"Oh, he's not so bad, once you get used to his manner."

"He seemed to . . . *resent* me." I'd been conscious of waves of hostility.

Terry laughed. "Nonsense, darling. You're imagining it."

But I wasn't.

A week or so later Uncle Ben who, as a bachelor, often had meals with us, brought Tom Baines along for supper. I'm certain Tom had solicited the invitation.

He quickly sensed the score between Gwen and me. She had taken badly to my friendship with Terry and put all sorts of obstacles in our path. She enlisted Daddy's aid, too: it couldn't be coincidence that so often he wanted me to work late on an evening when Terry was off duty.

I once asked Terry why Gwen should react like this.

He laughed and said: "The old green-eyed goddess."

"You mean she's jealous? Of *me?*"

"Why not? It's a well-documented situation: 'mirror, mirror on the wall, who is the fairest of them all?' *You* know."

Actually I don't think Gwen was too worried. Like most self-centred people, she saw what she wanted to see. She convinced herself that Terry would soon tire of me, I was so lacking in sex appeal.

But this evening Tom Baines shook her complacency. "You've a very choosy daughter, Mrs. Armitage," he said, wagging a nauseating finger at me.

"What?"

If Terry had been there, he would have passed it off; he could always get round Gwen with that smile of his. But Terry was out on a call. And I was struck dumb.

Tom said: "I could name half-a-dozen girls who would give their eye teeth for a proposal from Terry Kendall. But not Mandy here. She turned him down." There was one of these deathly hushes, then he added: "Am I putting my foot in it? Didn't you know?"

Daddy said quietly: "Matter of fact, we didn't. Is it true, Mandy?"

"Yes."

They were both staring at me, my father and my stepmother. Then Uncle Ben began to speak about angling, and the tension slackened.

But I knew that wasn't the end of the story.

The counter-attack began a few nights later, when Shelagh Carey was invited for supper. Actually that first occasion was probably a bow at a venture: I doubt if even Gwen could have foreseen all the consequences.

But, my God, Shelagh seized her opportunity. She had all her goods on display, and, you have to hand it to her, she had plenty to offer. That marvellous black hair and the big eyes and the eager smile. And a dress cut so low you thought they would pop out.

I'm in a minority of one about Shelagh Carey. They all rave about her—a splendid teacher, *so* good with the children, and such a nice nature, too, never an unkind word for anyone. For my money she's one great big fraud: shot through with ambition and ruthless as they come. But then I'm prejudiced. I'm Mandy Armitage, and everyone knows what an oddball I am.

That first night the ground was prepared. Gwen wasn't slow to build on it: twice in the next three weeks Shelagh was invited back. She gave Terry the works and he was utterly bowled over. It was a superb exhibition of how to catch your man without appearing to want him.

Yet she had misjudged her man. She saw in Terry the handsome young doctor, son of an eminent surgeon, with a bright future assured. She missed the weakness and the self-doubts. Well, she would learn.

As for me, once Terry came under Shelagh's spell, I was nothing again, I was the secretary, a piece of office furniture. He was shamefaced when he told me he'd fallen in love. I made it easy for him, didn't show the hurt I felt. After all, I had turned him down, hadn't I? So we remained friends. Occasionally he would absent-mindedly tease me about my glasses and my hair. But he didn't *see* me any more. I stopped using make-up, my ephemeral interest in clothes evaporated.

No, I hadn't loved Terry Kendall, his loss caused me none of the destructive grief the loss of Kenny Peterson had brought. All the same he had meant something to me. It had been fun while it lasted.

Celia's thirteenth birthday fell on June 20, a Sunday. Gwen invited some of her friends for tea that afternoon.

Well, "friends" is perhaps not the right word, unless you count Freda Landy and Helen Potts, eleven-year-olds from her class at school, who had to be invited or Celia would have boycotted the party.

But the other girls were from her own age group: Lesley Peterson (Kenny's sister), Janice Allen, Anne Ridley and one or two more. Although they had little in common with Celia, Gwen kept inviting them to the house on one pretext or another. It was her ambition to have Celia accepted by her contemporaries. The invitations were hardly ever returned. I happened to know that Lesley's birthday was the very next day; but Celia wasn't invited to any party *there*. The truth was these girls just didn't like Celia.

It was hard to like her. I had tried my best. As half-sisters there ought to have been some point of contact, but I never found it. As she grew older, Celia's oddness stood out more menacingly. She could be quite vicious when thwarted; and she had surprising strength.

Not that she was often thwarted. It had been Gwen's policy from the start to deny her nothing, a policy that was bound to be self-defeating. I blamed Daddy more: as a doctor he must have known the dangers, yet he kept aloof. I never met anyone to rival my father in shuffling off his responsibilities.

The girls arrived at two o'clock. The plan had been to go for a swim first and then have a picnic on the lawn. But it turned wet after lunch, so they had their party in the drawing-room, that ghastly museum piece Gwen was so proud of.

I spent the afternoon in my room trying to read the Sunday papers while the blast of pop records filled the house.

Gwen had invited Uncle Ben, Dr. Cohen and his insipid wife, Terry, and Shelagh to come at four o'clock for the cutting of the birthday cake. She always made a production of Celia's birthday.

It wasn't what you would call a scene of gaiety when I went in. Splinter groups had formed. Celia herself, attended by the faithful Helen Potts, was moodily teasing Bess, the Labrador. And in a corner Lesley, Anne and Janice were deep in a private conversation.

They were very bright, these three; I think that's why Gwen picked them out. She somehow hoped their intelligence would rub off on Celia.

I knew Lesley best of the three—both as Kenny's sister and because she was in my Sunday-school class—but found her the least attractive: she was too conscious of her own merits. Janice was probably cleverer, but less well organised. The star was Anne Ridley: she was very pretty, athletic *and* brainy.

Celia blew out the candles, we all sang "Happy Birthday," then the cake was cut and passed round, the Cokes were replenished (we'd ordered enough to float a battleship), and the adults had tea. Daddy drank his quickly and slipped out—back to his study to watch cricket on television.

I was about to go away myself when the incident happened.

Janice had been saying something—I didn't catch what it was —about the school, when Celia called out in a voice that silenced the rest of the room: "Of course, we all know why you get good marks in history."

"Who, me?" Janice said.

"Yes, you. Peeping Tom is potty about you." This was Tom Baines, the history teacher.

Janice coloured. "Don't be silly, Celia."

"He is too! He gazes up the stairs after you to see your knickers, and—"

Uncle Ben exploded: "Celia, that's enough!"

But she wouldn't be stopped: "—and I bet that's why you wear such short skirts!"

Janice did her thirteen-year-old best to turn a disdainful back on her accuser. She remarked to Lesley: "What can you expect from a pig but a grunt?"

I was watching Gwen's face: she looked furious. But all she said was: "Anyone want more Coca-Cola?"

Just then Terry and Shelagh arrived, dripping wet. They'd been walking in the rain. Shelagh had brought a present for Celia —a lovely little teddy bear.

And, of course, it was a winner: Celia was fonder of her cuddly dolls and furry animals than of any humans, except possibly Uncle Ben.

Her mood could change in a moment. Now she was all smiles. "I was only kidding, Jan," she said. Janice accepted the apology frostily.

The whole atmosphere of the party changed. Shelagh sparkled, Terry was full of jokes, and everyone brightened. Everyone except me.

But then I'm Mandy, no one expects *me* to scintillate.

CHAPTER 3

And so I come back to the night Janice Allen disappeared. It was July 8—less than three weeks after Celia's birthday party— and it had been the hottest day of the summer.

I spent the evening curled on a lilo in my favourite spot in the garden, almost out of sight of the house, a book in my hand, a transistor radio by my side. The heat of the sun and the drone of a lawn mower from somewhere down the avenue made me drowsy.

At half-past nine Terry came across the lawn from the house, with Bess fawning at his heels.

"Care to come for a walk, Mandy?" he said.

"What's wrong with Shelagh tonight?"

"She's got a cold."

"And Meg?"

"Never mind Meg. I'm asking you."

"No, thanks, Terry, I'm content where I am."

Did he really think I'd come running back whenever he snapped his fingers? After six months!

He sat down on the lawn beside me and moodily chewed a blade of grass. "Where is everybody?" he said.

"Daddy's golfing. Isn't Gwen—"

"No, I'm just back from Vine Street and I had to scrounge my own supper." His tone was accusing.

"My job is secretary, not cook."

"I'm not blaming *you*." He was in a pet because his meal wasn't on the table for him. And because Shelagh had let him down.

Bess nudged him with her nose.

"All right, all right," he said, getting up. "I'm coming." And to me: "Sure I can't tempt you, Mandy?"

I shook my head. He crossed the lawn towards the back gate, with Bess bounding ahead.

He'd seemed a bit depressed recently. He probably wasn't getting the sympathy from Shelagh he used to expect from me. Well, he'd made his choice. . . .

By ten o'clock the sun was low in the sky and the air was turning chilly. I went inside.

There was still no one at home. Gwen, I guessed, was out looking for Celia: even at supper she'd been fretting. And, indeed, now that I thought of it, I remembered hearing a car leave while I was in the garden.

In the last few weeks Celia had been encouraged to play tennis at Meadow Park. Uncle Ben had persuaded Gwen it would be good for her health—and, although I don't suppose he put it so bluntly, it was time to stop treating Celia like a baby.

Celia thrived on her extended freedom though I doubt if she played much tennis. She and Helen Potts and Freda Landy had other schemes for passing the time. If Celia wasn't home by nine o'clock, her mother was usually out looking for her, making herself a laughing stock. She'd never learn.

I made coffee and a sandwich and settled down to finish off Daddy's *Times* crossword. He was never very hot on the literary allusions.

At ten twenty-five the telephone rang. It was the wife of a patient wanting one of the doctors.

I said: "Dr. Radford's on call this evening." The operator should have put the call straight through to him.

"There's no reply from his number."

I was surprised, because Uncle Ben was meticulous about these matters. No use trying Dr. Cohen, who was on holiday.

"Well," I said, "you'd better ring the golf clubhouse. I think you'll get my father there."

It was now almost dark outside and I was becoming uneasy myself.

At ten-fifty Celia returned alone.

"Where have you been?" I asked.

"Wouldn't you like to know?" she said, smiling archly, and went upstairs.

Some time later Gwen came in. "Is she home?" she said.

"Yes."

"Thank God!"

I was almost sorry for her, she looked so haggard. Yet she was reaping what she'd sown.

If she would only, just this once, tear a strip off Celia, give her a real fright, put her across her knee, even, and tan the hide off her.

But no. She went up to Celia's room, there was a murmur of voices, and presently I heard Celia giggling. . . .

It was nearly midnight before Daddy returned. I knew from his wheezing that something had happened.

"There's a girl missing," he said. "Allen the chemist's daughter. She went swimming and she's not home yet."

"Oh no!" Gwen's hand went to her mouth and she turned pale. "It could have been Celia!"

Daddy poured himself a whisky and soda. "And the damnable thing is," he said, "I *saw* the girl. At least I think I did. If only I'd realised. . . ."

After his round he'd driven his golfing partner home to Moorend. When he came back by the coast road, it was dusk. Four girls, three of them wheeling bicycles, and all carrying bathing towels, were coming up the path from Abbot's Creek, just at the point where the road turned inland, skirting the golf course.

"The one without the bike was Janice Allen. I could have offered her a lift back, but I didn't think of it. . . ." He had returned to the clubhouse.

When Janice wasn't home by dark, her father contacted the parents of the three friends she'd gone swimming with. They were all safely home; they'd left Janice to walk home across the golf course.

Mr. Allen then rang the police. The first thing they did was to check if anyone at the club had seen the girl. That was when Daddy heard about it.

"There's a search party out now," he said. "I'd have joined it if I weren't so damned tired. And I'm a bit wheezy tonight." His tubes were whistling like an orchestra tuning up: he could produce the symptoms to order.

"Terry'll go," I said, and then: "Where *is* Terry?"
He wasn't home yet.

They found her clothes first, half buried in a bunker by the ninth green; and soon afterwards Janice's naked body, concealed under some whins nearby. It was three in the morning and the police doctor said she'd been dead about five hours. She had been strangled. There was no evidence of sexual assault: her clothes, it was believed, had been removed after death.

Chalford had more publicity in the next week than in the previous decade. Every newspaper you picked up had the story across its front page, usually with a picture of the ninth green and the whins beyond. On television Janice's face was the regular back-cloth to the newsreader's report.

In the town itself fear that the killer might strike again sharpened the sense of outrage. Parents took elaborate precautions to protect their children. Gwen wouldn't allow Celia to go out unescorted even by day.

A couple of days after the murder a police sergeant called at Tramore Avenue and took statements from all of us. I thought it was routine, a part of the house-to-house enquiry the police were supposed to be mounting. I had nothing useful to contribute.

Or so I thought. But next day I had a visit from Detective Inspector Hugh Robens, whom I knew personally. He was a member of our church.

He said: "One or two points arising from your statement, Mandy. . . ."

"Yes?"

"The night of the murder you were in the garden. Right?"

"Right."

"And Dr. Kendall came out and spoke to you?"

"Yes." I was beginning to see which way the wind blew.

"What time was this?"

"About half-past nine. I couldn't say exactly."

The inspector lit a cigarette; he'd been a non-smoker before he lost his only daughter from polio a couple of years ago.

"Was his manner normal, would you say?"

Normal? What was Terry's normal? He was so *volatile* . . .

"Yes," I said. "He was peeved because he'd had to make his own supper, that was all."

"Tell me exactly what was said."

I did. I've a good memory for the spoken word.

"And then he went off with the dog?"

"Yes."

"When did he come home?"

"About one o'clock."

"So he'd been walking three and a half hours? Didn't that strike you as odd?"

I shrugged. "He was often away for hours with Bess." I wondered if they knew about Meg.

He switched his ground. "I understand Janice Allen was a friend of your sister?"

Who had told him that? Gwen, probably. She liked to imagine that Celia was friendly with girls like Janice.

"Not a *friend,* exactly," I said. "A contemporary."

"But she did attend Celia's birthday party a week or two ago?"

"Yes." He was well clued in.

"Was Dr. Kendall there that day?"

"He looked in towards the end."

"So he'd met Janice?"

"Well, they weren't formally introduced. But he'd *seen* her, certainly." I added: "Terry's not your man."

"No? Well, then, he's nothing to fear, has he?"

They put the squeeze on Terry, grilled him daily for a week. The climax was a four-hour session at the police station on the Saturday, nine days after the murder.

Shelagh Carey was away that weekend. Visiting her mother, she said; but personally I suspected she was keeping out of the way while the heat was on Terry. She wouldn't want to commit herself.

Terry looked at the end of his tether when he came back from the police station. He had to talk to someone. He talked to me.

He told me he was under suspicion on three counts. First, by his own admission he'd been walking alone on the golf course about the time of the murder. Secondly, and more specifically, the three girls who'd been swimming with Janice had noticed him walking down the fairway towards the stile shortly after Janice left them. Yet he claimed he hadn't seen her.

"How could you have missed her?" I asked.

"She didn't come over the stile, I swear. And she wasn't on the road either, because I crossed the stile myself."

"Then where could she have gone?"

"Maybe she was picked up by a car. Or else she went back down to the beach for something she'd forgotten."

"Did you see any cars?"

"One or two passed. In fact—" He stopped.

"What?"

But he changed his mind. "No, it's nothing," he said.

"What were you doing down that way?" His usual rendezvous was the shed by the ninth green.

"I hadn't arranged to meet Meg that night—I had a date with Shelagh. But when she called off, and you wouldn't come for a walk, Mandy, I decided to try Meg's house. I'd remembered her mother was away."

"Did you see Meg?"

"Yes, I was with her for a couple of hours."

"Have you explained to the police where you were?"

"And risk losing Meg? Not likely."

"But she could *clear* you."

"Meg'll come forward if she has to. But not before. I haven't been charged yet."

"And meanwhile your story is you were walking the dog all that time?"

"They can't prove I wasn't."

For more than three hours, after dark? No wonder they didn't believe him.

"What's the third count?" I said.

"What?"

"You said they had three points against you."

"Oh yes. Well, you see, whoever killed Janice is obviously a psychopath. And they've discovered I once had a nervous breakdown. So there you are—it all fits: I'm a nutcase." He added: "The one bright spot is that Shelagh believes in me absolutely."

"I should hope so," I said tartly.

"How about you, Mandy? Do you believe me?"

"Of course!" If Terry had been guilty, he'd have cracked before now. Anyway, violence wasn't in his nature.

He was grateful. "It's done me good to talk to you, Mandy. You're just like my brother Mark—"

That did it. "Glad to have been of service," I said coldly. Like his brother Mark, indeed!

The pressure on Terry eased after that. Either he'd convinced the police he wasn't guilty, or at least they'd realised he wasn't going to crack.

No one outside our house—apart from Shelagh Carey—knew Terry was under suspicion. So once the police stopped crowding him, he was back to normal.

Back to *his* normal, that's to say. He still had his ups and downs. My impression was that Shelagh had little patience with his moods and already had misgivings about what she'd let herself in for.

She was often at Tramore Avenue, oozing charm. But occasionally I caught a speculative look in her eye. Terry had better not count his chickens. . . .

CHAPTER 4

I suppose one reason for the survival of the human race is its capacity to absorb and adjust to disaster. Even to forget.

There was a murderous psychopath at large in Chalford. All right, but you can't maintain a state of emergency forever, life must go on.

Perhaps he wouldn't strike again. Or if he did—well, there were fifty thousand people in Chalford, the odds against any particular one being the victim were comfortably large.

So as the long, hot summer passed, fear gradually receded, the pattern of life returned to normal. Children went swimming again. Not to Abbot's Creek—that *would* have been tempting providence; but the Pier sands were more popular than ever.

Gwen was one parent who didn't relax her guard: if Celia went out after tea, she had to have an escort. Often I was the chaperon. I would stretch out on the beach with a book and my transistor while Celia and her friends—the faithful Helen and Freda—fooled around in the water. I was appalled by Celia's treatment of these two girls: she bullied them constantly, making no allowance for the difference in age and strength. However, they survived and came back for more. Every sadist finds a willing victim. . . .

Terry and Shelagh had a couple of weeks in the Isle of Man in the second half of August. They returned bronzed and full of the joys, though there was no news yet of an engagement. Terry must still be on trial.

They described their holiday at supper at Tramore Avenue on their first night back. Clearly it had gone like a bomb. I guessed that Shelagh had slept with him, for she had that look on her face, like a cat that's been supping cream. And Terry looked pretty smug too.

After the superlatives were exhausted, Terry remembered to say: "How about you, Mandy? You go off next week, don't you?"

"Tomorrow."

"Where?" Shelagh asked.

"The north-west of Scotland."

"Oh how nice! Who with?"

"Alone." As if she didn't know!

"Oh! . . . Well, it should be marvellous up there in this weather."

It *was* marvellous, though the weather broke after the second day. I was youth-hostelling on a hired bicycle; and there was a perverse pleasure in slogging painfully over the remote, mountainous, rain-swept roads. I was Mandy Armitage, and to hell with the rest of the world! I was independent, self-sufficient, no one would ever hurt me again.

In Ullapool I was mending a puncture when a boy came over and offered to help. Nice boy, about my own age, shy, good-looking—reminded me a bit of Kenny Peterson. Afterwards he invited me to share his picnic lunch. He was interested, I could see that.

But I said no, I had to press on. I was Mandy Armitage. . . .

I returned in mid-September to a crisis. Something had gone seriously wrong with Terry Kendall.

I'd seen Terry in his blacker moods before, but this was different. He looked worried rather than depressed, he acted like a man wrestling with a problem that overshadowed everything else. He would hardly speak to any of us.

It was affecting his work; there was a fuss about some prescription he'd written. Once I came on Daddy and Dr. Cohen with their heads together, discussing it with anxious frowns. They shut up as soon as they saw me.

Shelagh Carey came to see me one evening when Terry was on duty in Vine Street.

"I'm worried about Terry," she said. "Have you any idea what's eating him?" Her pride must have taken some swallowing for her to ask me that.

"How should I know?" I'm pretty gauche in dealing with people I dislike: I find it hard to be polite.

"He has a great respect for you, Mandy. I just thought he might have said something."

"Well, he hasn't." And I wasn't going to ask him, either. I'd had Terry Kendall . . .

"It came on so *suddenly*," Shelagh said. "He'd been in great form ever since our holiday, then—just like that, you'd have thought we were strangers. And he absolutely refuses to discuss it."

"Well, I'm sorry, Shelagh," I said. "I can't help you."

She made no move to go. She said: "I expect you know Terry had been ill before he came to Chalford."

"Yes."

"Did you hear what was wrong?"

"A nervous breakdown."

"Yes. . . . Mind if I smoke, Mandy?"

"Go ahead." I gave her an ash tray.

She lit her cigarette. "He was in a bad way, apparently. Tom Baines says they were afraid for a while he might be going permanently insane."

"Baines!" I gestured my contempt.

Shelagh shook her head impatiently. "I don't like Tom, either. But it ties in with the pattern here, doesn't it? All these highs and lows. Terry's unbalanced, Mandy."

"So what?" In spite of myself I wanted to defend Terry; I hated to hear her dissect him like a laboratory specimen.

Shelagh tapped the ash from her cigarette. "I'm very fond of him," she said. (What a chilling phrase, I thought, when poor Terry was head over heels in love with her!) "But one must face facts. There's one plausible explanation for the state he's in."

"What's that?"

"Remorse."

"For what?"

"For murdering Janice Allen. The police still think he did it, you know."

"And you?"

"I try not to believe it," she said in a low voice.

"And what do you want from me?"

"Reassurance, I suppose." Her eyes were fixed pleadingly on mine.

Flattery was Shelagh's weapon. She used it to win popularity, she made people feel their opinions mattered.

It cut no ice with me. I said coldly: "Terry's no murderer, and you ought to know it, Shelagh."

She smiled then. "You've really helped me, Mandy. I can see why Terry thinks so highly of you."

I wanted to spit.

Afterwards I asked myself why she'd come. To pump me? Possibly. But could she really have imagined that Terry would confide in me?

No, it was more subtle than that. She'd already decided that

Terry, murderer or not, was too unstable for her. From now on she'd be back-pedalling for all she was worth, preparing to bow out gracefully. She couldn't ditch him immediately: that would be kicking a man when he was down, and Shelagh had her image to preserve. But meanwhile she was sowing the seed, so that when the time came, no one would blame her.

Well, as far as I was concerned, she'd wasted her breath. . . .

Not that I was concerned about Terry Kendall: he could go to perdition for all I cared. And if I said that often enough, I might even believe it.

But you can't contract out of life so easily. As the jaws of the trap prepared to close on Terry, I found I did care.

Patients were beginning to talk; I overheard them in the waiting-room exchanging notes about Terry. Trivial things they'd never complained of before loomed large now that they'd heard about that error in a prescription. And *how* had they heard of that? Someone must have been telling tales out of school.

And not only about the prescription. The rumour had spread that Dr. Kendall was the pervert who had murdered Janice Allen. . . .

I was aware also of secret conferences between the three partners. One day I tackled Daddy.

"All these meetings with Uncle Ben and Dr. Cohen," I said, "—it's about Terry, isn't it?"

When Daddy was embarrassed, he fixed his eyes on a point above your left shoulder. "His name has cropped up," he admitted.

"Daddy, he's ill—anyone can see that. Why don't you send him on leave for a week or two?"

"That's one of the possibilities we've discussed."

"What others?"

"I'm sorry, my dear, but it's *sub judice*."

He looked at his watch and moved away. If I'd tried to detain him, he'd have dredged up an asthmatic wheeze and produced his inhaler. When Daddy chooses to be evasive, you can't win.

So I went to Uncle Ben.

To those who didn't know him, Ben Radford, I suppose, cut an impressive figure. He was now in his mid-thirties, fair-haired, broad-shouldered, and with a confident, slightly bombastic manner.

But he was a phony. There was precious little behind the façade, he crumpled at the first sign of opposition. Also he'd been Gwen's lover, which in my eyes made him faintly ridiculous.

He had no scruples about discussing Terry. Dr. Cohen, he said, was pressing for his dismissal, although his contract had six months to run.

"On what grounds?" I asked.

"Negligence and incompetence. That prescription he wrote for Mrs. Phillips could have killed her if Allen the chemist hadn't been on his toes."

"Yes, but Terry's *ill*, Uncle Ben. He needs a rest, that's all."

"That's exactly what I've been saying, Mandy! Send him to a psychiatrist, I said. And if I hadn't spoken up for him, he'd be out on his ear by now. Though, mind you, your father's worried about the legal aspect—wrongful dismissal and all that." Yes, that sounded more like it: Daddy's caution would carry more weight than any advocacy of Uncle Ben's.

"Edward Cohen's consulting his lawyer," he added. "Of course" —he broke off and peered round my office as if there might be someone concealed under the desk—"there's more in this than meets the eye."

"What do you mean?"

"Well"—he spoke in a confidential whisper—"people are saying that Terry knocked off little Janice."

"What people?"

"You know how it is: just people in general. Not that I believe it for *one minute*. Not Terry . . . But all the same, once a story like that takes a grip, it's very bad for the practice. I do understand how your father and Edward feel about it."

"Well, I don't. I say to hell with rumour!"

"Ah yes, you were always out on a limb, weren't you? . . . But don't get me wrong, Mandy. I'm fighting tooth and nail for Terry. And the battle's not lost yet."

It was lost if Uncle Ben was Terry's only defender. So I did what I had vowed not to do. I tried to have it out with Terry.

He turned up half an hour late for evening surgery, and I smelt alcohol from his breath. It was, perhaps, significant that only a handful of patients had made appointments to see him.

When the last patient had gone, I went into the consulting room. "I think you ought to know," I said, "that you're in danger of being fired."

"I'm aware of it."

"Why don't you—"

" '—Pull yourself together?' " he completed the sentence for me. "I'm sick to death of that bloody phrase." It was clearly a reference to Shelagh.

"I was going to say: why don't you tell me what's worrying you?"

"Sorry, Mandy, I can't. . . . But I'll be all right soon. I've written to Mark."

Brother Mark. The oracle.

Terry needed someone to confide in, someone to put his problems in perspective.

Once I might have served, but not any longer. And Shelagh? Shelagh was ranged with the enemy: all she could say was 'Pull yourself together.'

"How's Meg?" I asked.

He frowned. "I haven't seen her. She's been away."

The following evening there was a dinner party at Tramore Avenue. When I heard who the guests were to be—Uncle Ben, the Cohens, Tom Baines and Shelagh—I cancelled my stint at the hospital and stayed home for the evening. Terry might be glad of one friend.

Tom earned his supper that night. On social occasions the Cohens are as silent as myself; and the rest of the company wasn't exactly scintillating, either. But Tom kept things going with his mildly scurrilous anecdotes.

Several of his stories were designed to illustrate his success with women. Despite that, I had a suspicion he was a homo. Nothing much to go on, really: just the way he spoke to me—with *dislike* rather than the usual indifference—and the way he looked at Terry.

I was in the kitchen getting the coffee when the telephone rang. I went out to the hall to answer it, but Celia had already lifted one of the receivers upstairs.

I heard her say: "Yes, I'll tell him," then she came running down in her dressing-gown, ignoring me, and burst into the dining-room. "That's a personal call for Terry," she said. "It's a *lady*."

Terry took the call in the hall, while I returned to the kitchen.

I overheard his side of the brief conversation. I suppose the others did too, for he'd left the dining-room door open.

"Tonight? God, yes, I'd love it! Usual place? Have to be latish, though. Half-past twelve? All right, I'll try. Bye."

I guessed that Meg was back. Terry was noticeably brighter for the rest of the evening.

When he left with Shelagh, she had that "I want a serious talk with you" look on her face, and I pitied him. The others had already gone.

Gwen, who had been quiet all evening, said she had a headache and went to bed. I talked to Daddy for a bit, trying once again to pump him about Terry. Although he was as evasive as ever, I had an intuition that Terry's fate was already decided and the chopper was about to fall.

When I pressed Daddy, he made his usual shameless use of his asthma. He said he felt an attack coming on and he'd need to get something from the surgery. So off he went and didn't reappear.

Mrs. Jackson, our daily, had already done most of the clearing up. I unloaded the dishwasher, tidied things away. Bed didn't attract me. I couldn't rest until Terry was home. So I got myself a glass of milk from the fridge and sat down in the drawing-room to wait for him. Daddy hadn't returned: he must have slipped up to his room.

At twelve-fifty I heard the back door open, a woof from Bess, then the door closed again. Hurrying through to the back, I opened the door and just caught a glimpse of Terry disappearing into the darkness with the dog.

His date with Meg must have been for tonight.

I went to bed and slept.

PROLOGUE TO PART II

It was nearly one o'clock when Terry Kendall went through the gate into the golf course. He hoped Meg had waited. He could never have foreseen that Shelagh would keep him so long.

Sometimes he wondered if Shelagh really loved him. She was so impatient of his moods and so ready with her advice: "Pull yourself together," "snap out of it." Easy to say. She didn't understand, she didn't *try* to understand.

Nor did she trust him. Despite all her protestations, he sensed a lingering doubt over the Janice Allen affair. She still thought he just *might* have done it.

But then who was he to complain, when he had the same agonising doubts? There were these two incidents, two pieces of evidence, you might say. The first he'd dismissed as a trick of the light, an optical illusion.

But the second incident wasn't as easily explained away. His eyes hadn't deceived him that time. Could it be coincidence, could there be an innocent explanation? Yes, just possibly, though the girl had been frightened, there had been fear in her voice. But he hadn't dared ask questions: he was afraid of the answers he would receive. . . .

For most people there would have been no problem. Go to the police, tell them what you saw, then leave it to them: it's their business, they'll decide. But informing the police was tantamount to an accusation; and Terry shrank even from formulating the thought in his mind, far less translating it into action. It was too horrible.

So he did nothing. But all the time this terrible load of guilt lay over him. Suppose there was a second murder: how would he feel then? Indeed, if he hadn't arrived on the scene just when he did that second time, would there already have been another death?

Mark would know what to do. He was so sane and sensible: worries seemed to melt away once you'd discussed them with Mark. You wondered afterwards why on earth you'd been in such a state.

But Mark was on the other side of the Atlantic. Terry had written him yesterday. He'd tried to set everything out on paper, but it looked so monstrous written down in cold blood that he'd scrapped the letter and begun again. This time he'd simply said enough to convey to Mark that he had a big problem.

Mark would read between the lines. He was due home in a week or two anyway. Maybe when he got Terry's letter he'd take an earlier plane. . . .

It was dark tonight, and Bess had run on ahead out of sight. She knew where they were going: they'd been this way many times before.

Terry was happier now that Meg was back. She knew how to cope when his spirits were low. None of the "Snap out of it" technique: just an extra gentleness.

He only hoped she'd waited. Half-past twelve, they'd agreed, and already, as he skirted the golf clubhouse and started the steep climb up the cliff path, it was ten past one. He shouldn't have gone home for Bess, he'd done that from habit. He just wasn't thinking straight these days.

He kept to the inside of the path, for on the left there was a sheer drop to the rocky beach below. Dr. Armitage had been campaigning for years to have the path fenced, but the council paid no attention. There hadn't been an accident there in living memory. Not yet.

The Devil's Shoulder formed a bulge at the highest point and appeared to lean out over the precipice. Here the path skirted even closer to the edge.

As Terry reached the shoulder, a figure loomed up in the darkness beside him.

"Meg!" he said.

But it wasn't Meg.

PART II

MARK KENDALL

CHAPTER I

The inquest had begun before I got there. They wouldn't let me in at first, until I told them who I was. I slipped into a seat at the side, laying my dripping raincoat at my feet.

The hall was set out as for a concert, with rows of canvas-backed chairs facing the platform. They had over-estimated the public interest: barely fifty spectators were huddled in the front rows. There was a smell of disinfectant and damp clothes.

On the platform the coroner sat at a table, flanked by his officials. Opposite him, in the witness chair, the pathologist was expatiating on the injuries and precise cause of death. My attention soon wandered. A smashed skull is a smashed skull. . . .

I wondered if Shelagh was here, tried to pick her out from Terry's description; long black hair, and a faint scar on her left cheek. Yes, that must be her, two rows from the front.

The girl looked up, briefly met my gaze, then turned away. She had a pleasant, unremarkable face; the large, dark eyes were the best feature. She didn't look Terry's type at all.

The pathologist stood down at last and Dr. John Armitage was called. A stout, balding man in a double-breasted grey suit stepped forward and took his seat at the table.

He was, he said, senior partner in the practice in which the deceased had worked. Dr. Kendall had come as an assistant eighteen months ago and he'd lived with the Armitages.

"His work was satisfactory?" the coroner asked.

"Yes, indeed. Entirely." Armitage's voice was rich and plummy: the bedside manner adapted to all occasions.

"He had no personal problems that you're aware of, Doctor?"

"No, Terence had everything to live for." He gestured vaguely towards the body of the hall.

He moved on to the events of last Friday. "We'd had friends in for dinner," he said. "The others left about half-past eleven, then Terence ran Shelagh—Miss Carey—home. I was in bed when he got back, but I heard him put the car away. Then he opened the back door and let Bess out."

"Bess?" the coroner asked.

"Our Labrador. Terence often took her for a walk last thing at night."

Armitage was wakened at four o'clock by a dog barking. It was Bess, alone. When he discovered that Kendall wasn't in his room, he raised the alarm. The body was found at dawn on the beach below the Devil's Shoulder.

"For years I've been urging the council to fence that cliff path," Armitage said. "But it takes a tragedy to—"

"Quite so, Doctor. . . . It was a dark night, wasn't it, on Friday?"

"Yes. Dry, but overcast."

"One last question. Had Dr. Kendall consumed much alcohol during the evening?"

"He had a glass or two of wine at dinner. But he was perfectly sober."

"Thank you."

The doctor nodded, left the platform and sat down in the front row of chairs. He took a handkerchief from his breast pocket and dabbed at his face.

Shelagh Carey had taken his place on the platform. She was wearing a dark blue midi coat. Her shape was good.

She described herself as a schoolteacher and said she'd known Dr. Kendall about six months.

"You knew him well?"

She hesitated fractionally. "We were good friends," she said.

Her voice was low and musical, with the faintest trace of an Irish influence.

She confirmed Dr. Armitage's account of last Friday's dinner party. Terry had driven her home. They talked for a bit, then he left about twelve-thirty.

"What sort of mood was he in?"

"Much as usual."

"You didn't gain the impression he was . . . depressed or upset?"

"Not at all."

The coroner persisted. "I mean, you hadn't quarrelled, for example?"

Shelagh said firmly: "No, we hadn't quarrelled. And if you're suggesting Terry might have committed suicide, I can assure you—"

"My dear Miss Carey"—he was smiling as he polished his gold-rimmed spectacles—"one has to ask these questions, if only for the record. . . . You've been most helpful."

She stepped down.

A police inspector gave evidence of the finding of the body and testified that the footpath along the cliff ran very close to the edge at the point where Dr. Kendall had fallen. Then it was all over, and the inevitable verdict of "death by misadventure" was reached; with a rider recommending that a fence be erected on the public footpath across the Devil's Shoulder.

As the hall emptied, I made my way towards the officials coming down from the platform. Shelagh Carey intercepted me.

"You're his brother, aren't you?" she said.

"Yes. Am I so like him?"

"No, but I guessed. . . ."

"He mentioned you, Miss Carey, in his letters."

"We were good friends." It was the slightly prim expression she had used in her evidence. Then she added abruptly: "I'd like to talk to you. But not here. Where are you staying?"

"The Lion."

"Will six o'clock suit? I promise not to stay long."

"Fine. I'll be in the bar."

She nodded and turned away.

The uniformed inspector was hovering. "You'll be Dr. Kendall, sir?" He was a big, soft-spoken man, with the build of a heavy-weight boxer.

"Yes."

"I'm Inspector Trapp from the local division." We shook hands. "We did our best to contact you, but we didn't know your address in the States."

"You did well to find me so soon." I'd got the cable yesterday morning.

"A sad business, sir. . . . There are no other relatives, I understand?"

"We have cousins in Canada, that's all."

"Just so. . . . We couldn't hold up the inquest—"

"No, of course not." Then, on impulse I said: "Inspector, are you *quite* satisfied it wasn't suicide?"

"Any reason why I shouldn't be?"

"No." Except for that final letter from Terry. But I didn't mention it.

The inspector's eyes were watchful. "Well," he said slowly, "you heard the evidence, you heard the verdict. I'm not God, I don't know what thoughts were in his mind when he fell. I doubt if it's profitable to speculate."

Let dead men sleep. No doubt he was right.

Dr. Armitage came over. "You must be Mark?" he said, pumping my hand. "Terence often spoke of you. I'm not interrupting, Inspector?"

Inspector Trapp smiled and walked away.

Now that I was closer, I was conscious of Armitage's asthmatic breathing. He'd need to watch his weight, too: he looked a front runner in the coronary stakes.

"You were very kind to my brother, Dr. Armitage."

"We all liked him." He shook his head and sighed. Then, more briskly, he said: "All his things are still at my house. I expect you'll want to . . ."

"Yes, of course, I'll get them cleared out." I was wondering if Terry had made a will. Almost certainly not.

"No hurry, my dear fellow. You must have a lot on your mind. When's the funeral?"

"I don't know yet. I'm looking for someone called Greene. . . ."

"The undertaker? That's him over there, talking to the coroner." A stout little man in a dark suit.

Armitage continued: "Have you made any arrangements, Mark, for tonight? Gwen and I could put you up if—"

"I'm booked in at the Lion."

He looked relieved. "But perhaps you'll have a bite of supper with us?"

Not the warmest of invitations, but I accepted it. "I'd love to. What time?"

"Ah yes. . . . Shall we say seven o'clock?"

We said seven o'clock. And Dr. Armitage looked at his watch, muttered something about calls and took himself off.

Hubert Greene had the undertaker's talent for euphemism. He discussed Terry's funeral with me without ever mentioning death or a body or coffin or hearse. We might have been arranging a sherry party.

It was all cut and dried: three-thirty tomorrow at the crematorium. The notices and the invitations were ready to go off as soon as the inquest was over.

"Who are the invitations going to?" I asked.

"Well, sir, we thought you'd want it to be a *quiet* occasion. Just one or two local friends and patients. And, of course, no doubt you'll have some names to give us."

Not very many. . . .

The little man coughed. "Would you wish to view the . . ."

"Body?"

"The *remains*," he amended reproachfully.

"Yes, please."

He brightened. "We've done a very tasteful job, if I may say so, sir. In the most *trying* circumstances."

He drove me to his funeral parlour.

Terry's face was scarcely marked. And they'd done something with his hair to mask the devastation at the back.

In death he had retained that look of youthful innocence which had been his great charm. And often his downfall.

I turned away from the coffin. I was angry at the futility of it all.

"Very peaceful he looks, wouldn't you say, sir?" The undertaker was hovering, rubbing his hands.

"Very dead," I said shortly. "How do I get to the Lion from here?"

Shelagh Carey came into the bar on the stroke of six. She peeled off a dripping P.V.C., revealing a dark green trouser suit. She was full-breasted, slender-hipped, long-legged. When she smiled as she crossed the floor to greet me, I began to understand Terry's superlatives. The smile transformed her face, lifted it out of the commonplace.

She chose a dry martini and I had a brandy and soda. Apart from two men propping the counter, the bar was empty. We sat at a table in an alcove.

Shelagh said: "So Terry mentioned me in his letters?"

"Yes."

"What did he say, exactly?"

"He painted a vivid pen picture, even to that scar on your cheek. . . . Where did you get it, by the way?"

She frowned impatiently. "Never mind that. . . . What else?"

"He said he was in love with you."

Silence while she sipped her drink and stared at me. She seemed to change the subject. "It's odd meeting you like this. You're not what I expected."

"What did you expect?"

"Well, from what Terry said, I pictured someone with a bulging forehead and thick glasses. The intellectual type. To be honest, you sounded a *drip*."

"And now you've met me, you've changed your mind?"

Those big eyes were still assessing me. "I'm not sure," she said. "Not altogether. . . . It's a pity you weren't able to visit him occasionally."

"I've been in the States for the last year."

"I know. But he needed you."

"What for?"

"As a sort of father figure, I suppose. To keep him on the rails."

"I'm three years younger than Terry."

"All the same, that's how it seemed to me."

It was a fair enough assessment of our relationship. Since our father died, Terry had turned to me whenever he was in trouble.

"I have my own life to lead," I said.

"I'm not blaming you. I'm only saying it's a pity . . . You see—" She hesitated. "He signed me on as a substitute, and I couldn't cope."

"But, Shelagh, even if I'd been here, I couldn't have stopped him from falling over a cliff."

She laid down her glass. "You might have stopped him from *wanting* to," she said.

"But the evidence this afternoon—"

She shrugged. "All rigged. John Armitage believes it was suicide, the police have a shrewd suspicion. And, God help me, I'm certain of it. . . . When did you last hear from Terry?"

"I got a letter yesterday morning." Only hours before the cable announcing his death.

"What was it like, that letter? Did he sound normal?"

"No," I admitted, "he didn't."

"We've all been worried about him," Shelagh said. "Of course, he was often a bit broody, though usually it didn't last long. But these last weeks he was *impossible*. John Armitage advised him to take a holiday. As for me, I kept telling him to snap out of it." The hand holding the glass was trembling. "That's all the comfort he got from *me*."

"Why did you say nothing of all this at the inquest?"

"What was the use? Besides—who knows?—perhaps it *was* an accident."

"Then why tell me now?"

She sighed. "When I saw you there, listening to these lies and half truths, I knew it wasn't right. We owed it to you to give you the truth."

Poor Terry! He'd talked about suicide more than once, but I

never really believed he would do it. I wondered what had finally pushed him over the threshold. Something quite trivial, possibly. I asked Shelagh if she knew.

"No, he wouldn't tell me." Her denial came a little too pat, but I didn't press her: Terry's reasons weren't important.

Shelagh said: "I failed him, Mark. I let him down when he needed me. . . . I wasn't patient enough. I was tired of his moods, sick to death of holding his hand and comforting him. I warned him that unless he mended his ways, we were through." She looked near to tears.

"Let me get you another drink."

She shook her head and stood up. "Thank you for listening," she said abruptly, and left me.

CHAPTER 2

The steelworks, the shipyard and the docks—that was Chalford. Even before I set foot in it I could have described the town, from the garish shopping centre to the rows of red-brick houses. I had seen so many like it in the industrial north.

It hadn't stopped raining since I arrived. As I paid off the taxi outside Dr. Armitage's house on Tramore Avenue, I had a brief impression of a wide, tree-lined street, solid houses and spacious gardens, then I was sprinting up the paved pathway to the shelter of the doctor's porch.

John Armitage took me into a square, high-ceilinged drawing-room, elegantly furnished, perfect but impersonal; like something out of *Ideal Home*.

A coal fire was burning in the grate—smouldering, rather: on one tiny yellow flame rested the only hope of warmth to come.

"Hellish weather," Armitage said. "First time in years we've needed a fire in this room in summer."

Summer, I thought, must run late in Chalford. We were nearly into October.

"Gwen'll be down presently. You'll have a sherry?" He filled a glass from a decanter.

From somewhere above a woman's voice called "John!"

"Damn!" he muttered. "You'll excuse me? Make yourself at home. That's the *British Medical Journal* over there."

He went out.

The *B.M.J.* was three weeks old, and I'd read it. The sherry was too sweet.

The door opened and a man came in. Middle thirties, fair hair, medium height, well built.

"You'll be Kendall?" he said. "I'm Ben Radford." One of the partners; Terry had mentioned him.

He poured himself a sherry. "Refill?" he said to me.

"No, I'm all right."

"Ah, take the chance. You won't get another." He topped up my glass. "My God," he added, "this room would freeze the . . ." He went over to the fireplace and applied his foot to the smouldering black lumps of coal. It didn't make much difference.

"Sorry about your brother," Radford said.

"Thanks."

"Damn bad luck. Though how he could—" He didn't finish the sentence. Instead he said: "So you're in the racket, too?"

"Racket? Oh, I see . . . Medicine. Yes, I qualified a couple of years ago."

"You've been abroad, haven't you?"

"Yes, I've just finished a year at Boston on a post-graduate scholarship."

"Doing what?"

"Neurosurgery."

"And now what?"

"Haven't made up my mind. Hyslop in Barts wants me back."

"Does he, by God? You must be good. Hyslop has standards." I shrugged. "I think I'd rather get into general practice." Radford helped himself to more sherry: this time I declined. He said: "Did Terry speak much about his life here?"

"His letters were never very informative."

"God knows why he stayed. He must have seen he wasn't going to get a partnership."

"Dr. Armitage said at the inquest he was doing a good job."

"Ah well! *De mortuis,* you know. . . ."

Just then the door opened and Armitage and his wife came in. A black Labrador was at their heels. When it saw me, it bounded over, growling with menace. Mrs. Armitage calmed the dog. "Bess always barks at strangers," she said. "But she's quite gentle really. . . . How nice to meet you, Mark. You don't mind if I call you Mark?"

Mrs. Armitage was years younger than her husband; she was, as I learned later, his second wife. She'd been an attractive woman and might still be if she hadn't tried to turn the clock back by overdoing the cosmetics.

She apologised for not being down to greet me; she'd been attending to her daughter, she explained.

She turned to Radford. "Ben, she's wheezing again tonight. I've had to send her to bed."

Armitage said: "Leave it just now, darling."

"But when Ben's *here* . . ."

"I'll go up and see her," Radford offered.

His partner was exasperated. "We've kept Mark waiting long enough."

"Would you, Ben?" she said, ignoring her husband.

Radford was away ten minutes.

"She's fine," he said on his return.

We moved into the dining-room: another superb room, perfect of its kind. And even colder.

A girl was standing at the window gazing out on the rain-swept garden. She turned round as we came in.

She looked about twenty. Her fair hair was swept back severely and caught in a pony-tail. Her pale, oval face was untouched by make-up, and she wore rimless glasses. Her dark grey pinafore dress did nothing to soften the general impression of severity.

"Mandy," Mrs. Armitage said, "this is Dr. Kendall—you know, Terry's brother. Mark, meet my stepdaughter."

"How do you do?" Her voice was cool.

Armitage said: "Mandy's our secretary. Don't know what we'd do without her, eh Ben?"

Radford agreed. Mandy smiled and said nothing.

The meal—grapefruit followed by cold meat and salad—was not calculated to warm us. We were offered nothing to drink.

Conversation was sticky. I did my best with Mandy, but it was uphill work. She answered mostly in polite monosyllables.

Her father helped out once or twice. "No, Mandy's never worked anywhere else. We keep urging her to spread her wings, but she prefers to stay in the nest, don't you, darling?"

"Yes, Daddy." She stared at her plate.

"Perhaps," I suggested, "there's a boy friend here?"

It was a mistake. "Plenty of time for *that*," Mrs. Armitage said, pursing her lips.

For a brief second Mandy's mask was down, I surprised a look of—what?—hatred, contempt, derision? Then she was all withdrawn again, and I wondered if I'd imagined it.

My God, I thought, what sort of family is this? How did Terry stick it so long?

Out of the blue Radford said: "John, did you know Mark wants to be a G.P.?"

Armitage's fork paused on its way to his mouth. "Really? Terence was always telling us you were bound for Harley Street, or a Chair somewhere."

"Terry was talking through his hat," I said.

Radford persisted. "We do have a vacancy, John."

"Yes." His tone was wary. "Of course, one would have to consult Edward." This must be Edward Cohen, the third partner.

"All right, let's do that. Ring him now."

I said: "I'm sorry, but I'm not interested. I've a few offers already."

"Where, may one ask?" Armitage sounded relieved.

"Two in London, one in Southampton."

"Ah well, we can't compete with the fleshpots of the south. But if you should change your mind, my partners and I would be delighted to offer"—he thought better of it—"would be delighted to enter into discussions."

After coffee I asked if I could look through Terry's things. Mrs. Armitage took me to his room.

"I'm sorry Mandy was so rude," she said. "She's a difficult girl."

I murmured something non-committal.

Mrs. Armitage went on: "Such an *unnatural* life—out every other night at that place, no friends of her own age . . ."

"What place?"

But she was conducting a monologue. "I've warned her, but she won't listen. She's always been a loner. Not like Celia, who makes friends so easily."

"What age is Celia?" I asked.

"She was thirteen in June. Poor child, she's not very strong." She sighed, then added briskly: "But I mustn't inflict our worries on you at a time like this. . . . Well, this was his room, Mark. I still can't believe he's gone. He was such a vital person. And always so *cheerful*."

Cheerful? She had totally misread Terry if she believed that: only the most superficial observer was deceived by his ready smile.

Unlike the rooms I had seen, Terry's was drably furnished. An ancient, elaborately carved double wardrobe and a dressing table of the same vintage dwarfed the modern divan bed. The pink motif of the wallpaper was fading to brown, the curtains were dark brown, the Indian carpet a dull grey. Terry's books—medical texts, science fiction paperbacks, one or two standard erotica— were on shelves along one wall. The only other immediate evidence of his occupancy was the writing desk which he'd lugged around everywhere and which had some sentimental value for him.

Mrs. Armitage said: "There's a trunk in the attic that's lain there since he came."

"I'll not bother with it tonight."

"His clothes are in the wardrobe. And you'll find most of his papers in that escritoire. If you want any help—"

"No, thanks, Mrs. Armitage. I'll just browse around on my own."

Still she lingered. "You're very like your brother," she said. Another misjudgment.

"No, I was the ugly duckling."

"Ugly? Oh no, I don't think so. . . . I'm sorry you're not accepting John's offer. You'd have liked it here."

I hadn't heard any offer from her husband.

When I didn't reply, she said: "Well, I'll leave you to it." But at the door she paused again. "Did you meet Shelagh Carey? She was at the inquest."

"Yes."

"They'd have made such a nice couple, Terry and Shelagh, don't you think?" She went out.

I hadn't meant to do more than glance over Terry's belongings, as a farewell gesture rather than from genuine interest in them. He had travelled light and gathered little moss. The clothes could go to charity, the books too, most of them, although one or two I might keep. Any papers and correspondence I'd pass to Rex Farrell, the family solicitor, to sort out.

But once I opened the writing desk, my interest was engaged. We'd never been close, Terry and I, our interests and personalities diverged too widely; but there was a bond. When he was in a fix, I'd cursed him but always helped in the end; while Terry in his curious fashion was proud of his more successful younger brother.

The contents of the desk, as I had expected, were in some disorder. But at least he'd kept his business papers in a separate drawer: bills, receipts, bank statements, dividend warrants. A cursory examination showed that he wasn't, as so often in the past, in a financial jam. He seemed to have several hundred pounds with a building society and a credit balance on his current account.

When he was a student, Terry had run up bills he couldn't pay, and Father had had to rescue him. He'd had extravagant spells since; usually it meant he was lashing out presents on some girl. He had no sense of proportion, that was his trouble. I'd been forever lecturing him about that.

It looked as if his sex life in Chalford had been less expensive. I couldn't see Shelagh Carey accepting presents beyond his means. But then Shelagh was out of the usual run of his girl friends. I doubted if she'd jump into bed whenever he whistled; or indeed if she'd jump into bed at all.

So where had Terry been getting his sex? He had a compulsive need for it. No doubt there was a local tart. . . .

I came across two letters from myself, written from the States. Remembering Shelagh's charges of priggishness, I read them over. Yes, they did sound a bit condescending. But how could I help it? Terry had been so exasperatingly irresponsible, one had always to be preaching.

The most recent correspondence was inside the roll top of the desk. It included a letter from Shelagh, dated September 21 (three days before Terry's death) which said:

> My darling Terry,
> Since you will not listen to me, I must spell it out on paper. Your continued moping is something, up with which I will not put, as the man said who refused to end a sentence with a preposition. I am *very, very* serious: snap out of it, or else! . . .
> Yes, I'll come to the Armitages' dinner party on Friday. You will be on trial; and it's your last chance.
> > Love,
> > Shelagh.

And, finally, an uncompleted airmail, dated September 23, and beginning "My dear Mark." This appeared to be a discarded version of the letter which had reached me just ahead of the news of his death.

I studied it as if it were a newly discovered Shakespeare text. In the letter I'd received in Boston the first page was devoted to the trivia of his daily round, then overleaf he plunged into his real reason for writing. I knew the passage by heart: "Mark, I wish like hell you were here. I'm sitting on a bomb and I haven't the guts to tackle it alone. When are you due back, Mark? It's soon, isn't it?" End of letter.

The draft I was now looking at began where the other one ended: "Mark, I wish like hell . . ." But then followed a new paragraph: "One night—a week ago last Tuesday—I saw something, innocent in itself, but if you relate it to what happened earlier—No, I can't bring myself to put it down on paper, it's too horrible, it *must* be false. . . . Yet I can't leave it there, for it does tie up with what I thought I saw last July. Suppose it were true—what a load to have on my conscience! Twice I nearly questioned the girl—when I saw her next day and again when she came to the surgery last night."

The draft stopped there. Terry must have decided he'd said too much, he'd have to wait till I got back (it would have been about ten days). But after all he hadn't waited: the strain, whatever it was, had become more than he could bear. It was always on the cards: his tolerance of stress was abnormally low.

The letter was still in my hand when there was a knock on the door and John Armitage came in.

"Still at it?" he said.

"I'm sorry, I'm imposing—"

"Not a bit. I've some work to do in my study, but Gwen'll get a drink before you go."

"Thanks."

"Everything shipshape?" He was given to clichés.

"I think so . . . Tell me, Dr. Armitage, was Terry very depressed latterly?"

"Depressed? We all have our ups and downs, don't we? But Terence had everything to live for."

He had used that phrase before. "What, precisely?"

He frowned. "Well," he said, "Shelagh Carey for a start. A splendid match."

"But they weren't even engaged."

"Not formally. But there was an understanding."

"That's not the impression I got from Miss Carey."

"Oh really? . . . Well, I mustn't hold you back." He was already edging out.

Terry was cremated the following afternoon. When I got back to the Lion after the service, the receptionist gave me a letter addressed in pencil capitals to "DR. MARK KENDALL." Inside, on cheap paper, was the message, also in pencil capitals: "YOUR BROTHER DIDN'T FALL, HE WAS PUSHED." It was unsigned.

There was no stamp on the envelope. The girl at the desk told me it had been put through the letter box.

I rang Shelagh Carey and told her about it.

"Ignore it, Mark," she said. "It's just some crank."

"Probably. But I can't *ignore* it. I must let the police see it."

Long pause, then: "I suppose so. But you'll only get hurt. There are things about Terry it's better not to know."

"What things?"

But she wouldn't say any more.

I cancelled my taxi, cancelled my sleeper, booked in at the Lion for a further night. Then I walked round to the police station.

Inspector Trapp was not on duty. A uniformed sergeant passed me on to the C.I.D.

Detective Inspector Hugh Robens was a thin, restless man of about forty, a chain smoker, to judge by the state of his fingers and the number of stubs in his ash tray.

He listened to my story, examined the anonymous note without enthusiasm.

He said: "Yes, well, this sort of thing's not unusual. There are people with sick minds—but you must know all about that, Doctor."

"All the same, it *could* be genuine."

He shrugged. "We'll investigate it. But take my word, if anyone *really* had evidence that your brother was murdered, he'd come and tell us instead of sending you a stupid message like that."

"What about this, then?" I handed him the draft letter I'd found in Terry's desk.

He barely glanced at it. "We've seen that."

Of course. The police were bound to have looked through Terry's papers after his death.

"Doesn't that suggest a motive?" I said. "He had some dangerous knowledge, so he was silenced." I didn't believe it myself, but was irritated by the inspector's total lack of interest.

Robens lit a cigarette. "Look, Dr. Kendall, the verdict was death by misadventure. Why don't you leave it there?"

"Because if he was murdered—"

"He was not murdered. We're very sure of that."

"Then how do you explain that letter he sent me?"

"That letter he *didn't* send you. He left it in his room where it would be found after his death."

"You think it was a suicide note?"

"*If* he committed suicide, yes. But I'm content to accept the jury's verdict. I think you should be, too."

But my mind was still on Terry's letter. "It's a curious suicide letter. He only hints at what was bothering him. Aren't they usually more explicit about their reasons?"

The inspector drummed his fingers on the desk. "The one thing every suicide wants to do is to justify himself, even if it means concealing the real reason for killing himself."

"You believe he had a different reason?"

"I'm not saying that, sir."

But he was. The police knew something about Terry that I didn't.

"Inspector, what the hell is all this mystery?"

"Mystery? I don't understand."

He did understand, but he wasn't going to tell.

He said formally: "Thank you, Dr. Kendall, for coming to see us. We'll investigate the matter. . . . Oh, and would you mind if we took your fingerprints?"

"What?"

He indicated the anonymous note. "A process of elimination. Not that we're likely to trace the writer that way."

I lay awake that night in the Lion long after the rumble of traffic on the High Street had stilled.

I'd always hated loose ends. Terry was dead: all right, I grieved for him, but I would adjust. His death was accidental, the jury said; not so, he killed himself, Shelagh Carey said, and the police implicitly agreed with her. I could adjust to that too.

But why had he done it? Terry had been depressed before now, had talked of "ending it all"; but he had never translated threat into action. What was the overwhelming motive that drove him this time beyond the point of no return? A motive that Shelagh knew of, and the police, but wouldn't reveal to me.

Also there was that note: "Your brother didn't fall, he was pushed." Melodramatic, spiteful, the work—almost certainly—of a diseased mind. Yes, but just *suppose* . . .

By morning my mind was made up. I rang Ben Radford before breakfast.

"Dr. Radford," I said, "were you serious yesterday when you suggested my joining the practice?"

"My God, yes! Have you changed your mind?"

He contacted his partners, and I met all three doctors that afternoon.

John Armitage was unenthusiastic. He pointed out the disadvantages of Chalford for someone like me: a "medical backwater" was how he described it. I wondered if my record frightened him and if he was happier working alongside mediocrity.

Although Radford was on my side, he was not a good advocate. He clearly didn't carry much weight with the other two.

By far the most impressive of the partners was the youngest, Edward Cohen, tall, earnest, bespectacled, silent. He listened to what his partners had to say, then announced that he'd rung two of my old professors that morning.

"My opinion is," he said, "that we should be extremely fortunate to have Dr. Kendall join us."

That settled it, apart from some bickering over terms. It was agreed that I should start as assistant in the practice at the beginning of October.

John Armitage was magnanimous in defeat. "I do hope you'll take Terence's room. It's so convenient to have our assistant staying in the house and you made a most *favourable* impression on my wife and daughter the other evening."

"That's very generous of you," I said.

He then told me the rent. I revised my opinion of his generosity.

CHAPTER 3

The main surgery was in an annex to Dr. Armitage's house on
Tramore Avenue. It contained a couple of well-equipped consulting rooms, a large waiting room and an office for the secretary.

I saw my first patients, however, in the Vine Street surgery at
the other end of the town. This was a depressing place, ill lit,
inadequately heated, and with only the barest minimum of fa-
cilities.

Dr. Armitage never darkened the Vine Street door. His two
partners and the assistant (myself) were supposed to take an equal
share in providing a nightly surgery; but I soon found out that the
assistant was more equal than the others.

One night during my first week a man, pushing thirty, tall,
dark, with a trim little moustache, came into the consulting room.
His lounge suit and minor public school tie set him apart from the
other patients I'd seen in Vine Street.

"Name, please," I said mechanically, stretching towards the
records cabinet.

"Don't you remember me, Mark?"

The voice brought it back, that slightly nasal drawl. He'd been
a friend of Terry's in London.

"It's Tom Baines, isn't it?" The moustache was new, that was
what had thrown me.

"Got it in one."

"We don't seem to have a record card—"

"Oh, I didn't come to *consult* you. Just to offer condolences
about Terry. And to ask you for a drink when you're finished
here."

I joined him in the Greyhound at half-past eight. He had a double
whisky waiting for me.

After coming down from Cambridge, Tom Baines had read for

the Bar. Or perhaps that's putting it too charitably. He dabbled with his legal studies and put most of his energies into left wing politics and a rather bohemian social life. Terry met him at a party somewhere and was enormously impressed.

To the end of his life my father blamed Baines for subverting Terry, laid at his door the drinking and the debts and the women. But the weakness was there in Terry, he was going to break out someday; if Tom hadn't been around, he'd have found some other avenue.

All the same, for two or three years they were very close. Then Baines gave up his pretence of study and left London. To do what?—I couldn't remember. He used to talk about a career in the Diplomatic Service but his Cambridge degree wasn't good enough for that.

"What brings you to Chalford?" I asked him.

"I'm a teacher. I live here."

"But why Chalford?" The place didn't fit him: he was metropolitan by birth and inclination.

"Why not? There was a vacancy."

"Was it Terry who suggested it?"

"Heavens, no! I was here long before Terry. It was the other way round, as a matter of fact. I put Terry on to Ben Radford. . . . Cigarette?"

"I don't, thanks."

He laughed. "Same old Mark! Still no vices? I often wondered what made you tick." He lit his cigarette. "I still do. Right now I'm wondering why you're slumming in Chalford."

"Same reason as yours. There was a vacancy."

"Won't wash, boy." He was still grinning. "Me, I had no option. As an ex-Party member, and with a lousy Third in history, I was almost unemployable. . . . But you could have had your pick: distinction in your finals, Ferncliffe Scholarship to Boston—I got the whole citation from Terry."

"I wanted to try general practice."

"No one in his senses would throw in his lot with Armitage and Radford if he had any choice. . . . Come clean, Mark: what's the game?"

His glass was empty. I finished my own drink and crossed to the bar for refills, wondering why Baines was so concerned.

When I got back, I said: "Did you see much of Terry after he came up here?"

He shrugged. "We had the odd booze-up. But not often. Terry had other fish to fry."

"You mean Shelagh Carey?"

"Yes. More fool he. I warned him he was tying a noose round his neck."

"You don't like her?"

"Not much. She's a colleague of mine at school, so I know her quite well. She's the *marrying* type. I always give them a wide berth."

"How's Norma?" I asked.

"Norma?" He looked blank. Then: "Oh Norma! God, I hadn't thought of her in years."

"You didn't marry her, then?" They'd been engaged when I last knew him.

"No, I escaped."

"And you're still single?"

"That's it. Still running." He lit another cigarette from the stub of the last one. "You haven't answered my question: why did you take a post in Chalford?"

"I'm not satisfied with the inquest verdict," I said, trying to gauge his reaction.

He expelled smoke through his nose. "Ah, so that's it! You're dead right, of course—it was no accident."

"How can you be so sure?"

"Because if ever I saw a potential suicide, it was Terry. Besides, unless he was tight, he'd never fall over that cliff without meaning to."

"Not even in the dark?"

"No. Go and have a look and you'll see what I mean."

"Any idea why he should kill himself?" I asked.

He didn't answer directly. "Have you been to the police?"

"Yes."

"Did *they* not suggest a motive?"

"No, but I got the impression they knew of one."

He grinned. "Too right they do."

"What's that supposed to mean?"

"Ah no, Mark! If they wouldn't tell you, damned if I will. It's only a bloody rumour anyway."

"I'd like to hear it."

He shook his head. "Forget it, Mark. So he killed himself: you can't bring him back."

"But suppose he didn't. Suppose someone *pushed* him over that cliff. . . ."

He stared at me. "You're not serious?"

"I'm not sure." I told him of the anonymous letter.

"What do the police think of that?"

"Not much."

Baines stroked his moustache. "I'm not surprised. Why should anyone want to do in old Terry? A more harmless—"

"Perhaps he knew too much."

"About what?"

"I don't know. Did he talk much to you, Tom? About himself, I mean?"

"It was his favourite subject."

"I'm told he was very depressed just before his death."

"Well, there you are: doesn't that suggest suicide?"

"Yes, but what was worrying him? Did he tell you?"

"When he was in his blacker moods, Terry never talked about it. He'd put a face on it and pretend there was nothing the matter. The smiling sickness, don't they call it? Though I confess he wasn't smiling much that last night."

"What last night?"

"The night he died. I had dinner at the Armitages'. Terry hardly uttered. In fact, none of them did. It was like a bloody wake." Briskly he changed the subject. "Now let's hear all about you, Mark. Terry told me you had a disappointment?"

A disappointment? Well, that was one way of putting it.

Mrs. Armitage asked about Zelda, too. At lunch one day she said, out of the blue: "Mark, whatever happened about that girl you were going to marry? Terry used to speak of her."

They were all looking at me. Gwen Armitage had a talent for creating embarrassment: she was abnormally insensitive to other people's reactions.

"Zelda?" I said. "She jilted me."

"What's 'jilted'?" asked Celia, the thirteen-year-old, whose vocabulary had many gaps.

"Left him at the altar," her father explained.

Celia thought about it, then giggled. Mentally she was slightly retarded, and Ben Radford had told me that at school she was two forms behind others of her age. This perhaps explained, though it hardly excused, her appalling behaviour, which went unchecked except—occasionally—by her stepsister.

It was Mandy who said now: "There's nothing to laugh at, Celia."

Celia stuck her tongue out, and Mrs. Armitage said: "Don't be such a prune, Mandy. Mark doesn't mind, do you, Mark?"

"No," I said.

Actually I didn't mind much. Zelda's name had lost the power to hurt.

I could tolerate the Armitages in small doses. John was the least complicated: a good enough doctor, but lazy, and something of a hypochondriac. He wasn't pulling his weight in the practice.

However, at least he left me alone. He would go off to his study after supper each evening, ostensibly to work on some article for *Lancet,* but in fact to watch television.

Mandy also disappeared as soon as the meal was over—either upstairs to her room or out in her Volkswagen. She did voluntary work two nights a week at the spastic children's hospital in Moorend; and she was also involved in various church organisations. An utterly colourless and uninteresting person.

Celia's bedtime was nine o'clock. Which left Gwen and me. She made me call her Gwen: Terry had, she informed me.

I sat with her most evenings in that chilly drawing-room. Unless I was going out, there was no alternative really, for my room had no heating at all.

Up to a point it suited me well enough, for Gwen would talk almost non-stop, and occasionally I could direct the flow with a discreet question. She wasn't, unfortunately, a good judge of character—she was too egocentric for that—but reading between the lines I learned quite a lot.

Her marriage, I gathered, was held together only by convenience. She and her husband had little in common and no longer even shared a room. There had been a big row ten years before when John had wanted to get rid of Ben Radford, whose contract as assistant was running out. Somehow Gwen bullied her husband into taking Ben into partnership.

She had an enormous regard for Radford, far beyond his real worth as a doctor. She maintained he was the only man who understood and sympathised with the problems of bringing up Celia; and that was all that mattered.

Gwen's whole life revolved round her daughter, and she deceived herself all the time—about Celia's health, her behaviour, her mental capacity. The girl she described and the girl I saw every day at meals were two different persons.

When Gwen spoke of her stepdaughter, which was seldom, her intense dislike shone through unmistakably. It surprised me that a girl as dull as Mandy could arouse strong feelings in anyone.

About Terry I learned little that was new. Except that he'd regularly taken the dog for walks at night and was sometimes away for a couple of hours. Since Terry had never been fond of physical exercise, I wondered if it had been an excuse to escape from Mrs. Armitage.

And perhaps it wasn't such a bad idea. By the end of my second week at Tramore Avenue I was almost at screaming stage, Gwen's monologues were so endless and so repetitive. So one night I asked if I could walk the dog. Bess, who had by now accepted me, indicated her approval, and off we went.

I took her to the edge of the common before letting her off the lead. She set off purposefully over the grass, wriggled under the fence onto the golf course and waited till I had come through the gate. Then she made off into the darkness while I followed the tinkling of her collar. She never paused and seemed to know exactly where she was going.

We crossed the first fairway past the clubhouse, then we were climbing the public footpath on the perimeter, just out of bounds. Far below us the sea shimmered in the moonlight and from time to time there were glimpses of the lights of the town.

At the highest point an outcrop of rock—known locally as the Devil's Shoulder—formed a kind of platform. Standing on it, looking out to sea, was like standing on the bridge of a ship.

Although the path followed the contour of the ground, it didn't come as dangerously close to the edge as evidence at the inquest had suggested. I'd been here before in daylight, and now, even in darkness, it was hard to understand how anyone could have fallen over. The stony path was sunk several inches below the ground on either side and there was a ledge at least two feet wide between the path and the edge.

Bess hadn't stopped on the shoulder and was already out of sight and earshot. She was waiting for me down the far side. When she heard me approach, she abandoned the path and struck out across the golf course to a wooden hut set in a sheltered dip and hedged on three sides by gorse bushes. On the fourth side a rough track led from the door of the hut towards a fairway.

It was, I guessed, an equipment shed for the grounds staff. Bess stood at the door wagging her tail. I tried the handle but it was locked. There was no window, and in any case it would have been too dark to see in.

Bess was sniffing around expectantly.

"She'll not be here tonight, Bess," I said. We set off home.

I spoke of it to Ben Radford next day.

"Just off the ninth?" he said. "Yes, that's where they keep some of their gear, to save them lugging it over from the clubhouse every time."

"What's it like inside?"

"How in God's name should I know?"

"My guess is that Terry entertained there."

"What?"

"Girls."

"Oh, I see. You don't mean Shelagh Carey, do you?"

"No."

"Because she's not that type."

"I know. But that's probably why he *needed* that type."

We were having coffee in the office after morning surgery. I could hear Mandy Armitage tidying the waiting-room.

After a long pause Radford said: "Take my advice, Mark, and lay off. You're stirring up an anthill."

"That's the general idea."

"You won't like what you find."

"That may be."

He was suddenly angry. "Damn it to hell, Mark, we all know Terry's death was no accident. They hushed it up at the inquest—did you ever ask yourself *why?*"

"You tell me."

"To spare his reputation, that's why. And if you go poking around—"

"All I want is the truth. What are you hiding from me, Ben?"

But, of course, he wouldn't tell me, none of them would tell me.

I even asked Edward Cohen. He listened gravely, then told me he knew nothing beyond what he'd read in the press.

"You must understand," he said, "that I didn't know Terence well. We had no *social* contact, as it were."

That I could believe. Cohen was too wrapped up in work and in his young family to have much of a social life. And in any case he had nothing in common with Terry.

He added: "His work had fallen off, that I can say. I was concerned about it. I advised John to terminate the contract."

"As bad as that, was it?"

"Frankly, even at best your brother was second-rate. And when he began to slip—I'm sorry, but one can't afford sentiment when patients' lives are at stake."

Poor Terry! I wondered if John Armitage had passed on the warning.

"But you've no idea, Edward, exactly what was upsetting Terry?"

The owlish glasses stared at me in surprise. "No, I've already told you, I scarcely knew your brother. We never discussed personal matters."

So Cohen didn't know, and the others wouldn't tell. I was driven back to Terry's letters, to the one I received in Boston and the uncompleted draft I'd found in his desk.

And I read again the sentence: "Twice I nearly questioned the girl—when I saw her next day and again when she came to the surgery last night."

CHAPTER 4

It was a Thursday morning and I was on surgery with John Armitage. As usual, he was away long before me: he always had a shorter list, and he gave each patient less time as well.

I was through by eleven o'clock and went into the office, where Mandy was pouring my coffee. She was efficient as clockwork, silent as a mouse, entirely self-contained. I'd long since abandoned any attempt to draw her out. It wasn't worth the effort: I'd have got a warmer response from a computer.

She never stayed to have coffee with me. Today she was slipping out as usual when I called her back.

"Mandy," I said, "could you find out for me whether my brother was on duty here or at Vine Street on the evening of September 22?"

Showing no surprise at my question, she produced a diary from her desk and flicked through it.

"He was here," she said when she'd found the page. "He and Dr. Cohen were consulting. Dr. Radford was at Vine Street."

"And would you still have his appointments for that evening?"

This time she took a file from a cabinet and handed me a sheet containing a list of patients' names, with the times of their appointments from 6 P.M. onwards.

Twelve patients, eight of them men. And of the women I knew two, both married, both middle-aged.

I asked about the other two. "Who are Miss Pearce and Mrs. Ellison? Have I seen them?"

"I don't think so. Miss Pearce is over sixty—"

"Forget her, then. What about Mrs. Ellison? What age is she?"

"Early thirties, I'd guess."

Could Terry have described her as a girl? Just possible, I supposed.

"Get me her file, would you, Mandy?"

She produced it.

Mrs. Ellison was thirty-four and expecting her third child. Yes, there was Terry's note: routine check-up because she'd suffered from hypertension during her last pregnancy. All right so far this time.

But I just couldn't see Terry describing her as "the girl."

I said to Mandy: "If another patient called that night—I mean, without an appointment—would you fit her in?"

"Provided we weren't running too late."

"But you'd have no record?"

"Not on our appointments list. But your brother would put a note on her card, presumably."

Yes, but we had four thousand patients on our list. Which meant four thousand cards.

Mandy said: "Is this important, Dr. Kendall? To find out who it was?"

"I think it might be."

She looked at me, expecting an explanation, but I didn't offer one. Finally she said: "I'll go through the cards this afternoon."

"But it's your half-day, Mandy."

She shrugged. "I'm not doing anything special."

"We'll do it together, then."

We examined the record cards of every female patient between the ages of five and thirty. On my own it would have taken hours, but Mandy worked like a computer. We'd started at two o'clock, and by half-past three we were finished. And had drawn a blank: we found not a single card on which Terry had made an entry on September 22.

"Are you sure you didn't miss any?" I asked.

She ignored the question. "Perhaps the girl didn't come about herself," she said.

"I don't follow."

"Well, she could have been getting a prescription for someone else in her family."

It was a possibility. "But if that was it, we'd have to look at every single card."

"Not necessarily. There aren't so many who send other people for their prescriptions."

She frowned in concentration, then began picking out individual cards and examining them. The fourth or fifth one she tossed over to me.

"There's your man," she said. "Harold Peterson."

He'd had a long history of illness, mainly from a duodenal ulcer, and there were three closely written cards stapled together. The penultimate entry was in Terry's handwriting: it was dated September 22 and recorded the renewal of three prescriptions.

"There's a daughter, is there?" I asked.

"Two daughters, but the older one's away nursing. I remember the younger girl, Lesley, coming in around that time. Her father's ulcer had been acting up and he'd been off work. The doctors visited him once or twice, but I'm sure he never came to the surgery."

"What age is she, this girl?"

"She was thirteen in June."

"You're a marvel, Mandy. How do you carry all that in your head?"

"I used to know the family." Her tone was distant again. She was, I could see, about to take her leave.

But I owed her an explanation. I said: "My brother wrote me a letter just before he died. He mentioned this girl he'd seen in the surgery."

"What about her?"

"Well, apparently she *knew* something that he found disturbing."

Mandy's eyes were on me, expressionless behind the glasses. "I don't understand," she said.

I tried again. "Did you notice any change in Terry in the last week or two of his life?"

"Yes. He was worried. He looked ill with worry."

Worry, she said: the others called it depression. The two were not synonymous.

"When you heard he'd been killed, what did you think?"

"I was extremely sorry—he'd always been considerate to me." The formal words rang hollow.

"I meant, were you satisfied it was an accident?"

There was a pause before she said: "What else could it have been?"

"Well, some people are saying it was suicide."

"What people?" I had touched off the first natural response.

"Shelagh Carey for one. And she knew him very well."

Mandy hesitated again, then said in her flat voice: "Yes, she did, didn't she?"

There had been just a flicker of animation on her face. She didn't like Shelagh, obviously. But that was to be expected. A girl like Mandy, unattractive, lonely, introspective, was bound to be jealous of those whom nature had more generously endowed.

And yet she didn't have to be quite so unattractive. It was partly the way she dressed, and the absence of make-up, and these awful glasses. Yes, and the hair style.

I was really seeing Mandy for the first time, seeing her possibilities.

I said: "Why do you hide your light under a bushel, Mandy?" I wanted to arouse some emotion in her, even if it was only anger.

"I beg your pardon, Dr. Kendall?"

It was the freeze-out, but I ignored it. "God meant you to be pretty. I'm surprised Terry never told you that."

Her cheeks turned scarlet, and behind the glasses her eyes flashed angrily. She walked out without a word.

It wasn't often I was goaded into such an indiscretion. In fact, Zelda used to complain of a lack of spontaneity: she said I weighed every sentence as if I feared a slander action.

But Mandy's aloofness had finally got under my skin. I felt she despised me; it was a new experience, and one I didn't enjoy.

At supper that night John Armitage said: "What kept you two occupied in the surgery all afternoon?"

"I was doing my homework on the case records."

"Why?"

Gwen answered for me. "Because Mark's conscientious, that's why. You're lucky to have him."

"Indeed, indeed, I count my blessings. . . . And what about you, Mandy? Giving up your half-day—"

"I was helping," Mandy said shortly.

"I bet you were snogging," Celia sniggered.

This was too much even for her mother. "Please, Celia, that's not very *nice*. . . ." All the same she rounded on Mandy. "Darling, have you been using my eye-shadow again?"

I'd been wondering what was different about Mandy this evening. I saw now she had put lipstick on too. It helped, but not enough to cancel out the hair and the glasses and the dowdy dress. If this was the result of my words today, I regretted them even more.

Mandy said: "It's not your eye-shadow, Gwen. I bought it for myself."

Gwen smiled gently. "My dear child, I've told you before, you're only asking for another of these allergies. Isn't she, John?"

"Yes."

"And anyway your kind of face is better without make-up."

Mandy retreated behind her wall of silence. But I saw that her hand was tightly clenched.

John Armitage turned to me: "Any special cases you were interested in, or were you just browsing?"

I said: "Wouldn't that chap Peterson be better to have an op.? With his record—"

"Oddly enough, Mark, the thought had occurred to us. . . . My God, man, maybe I didn't graduate yesterday, but I'm not from the horse and buggy era." He was very touchy about his professional competence. And indeed he was quite good; his main fault was indolence.

"I wasn't criticising," I assured him. "He funks it, I suppose?"

"Yes, we've been pressing him for years. You're welcome to try your luck if you want."

"He's back at work now, is he?"

"Yes. Till the next time . . ."

"I'll look in on Saturday."

Harry Peterson was sitting by the kitchen fire, reading his *Daily Express*. A gaunt man in his forties, with the pinched look of the chronic dyspeptic.

He was delighted to meet the new doctor, he told me. My brother had been good to him. So had all the doctors, he liked them all.

"You don't take their advice, though," I said.

He looked sheepish. "Oh you mean about the operation? Well, the day'll come, maybe. . . . But I'm fine now, never been better. Haven't been sick for days."

It was not the time to urge an operation on him. Get him when he thought he was dying.

I asked about his family. He had a son of twenty at the University of York, a daughter of seventeen, training to be a nurse. And Lesley, aged thirteen.

"Where's Lesley today?" I asked.

"Playing hockey. Then she'll spend the rest of the day with a school friend. We'll not see her till dark." He shook his head. "I worry about that girl when she's out late. Especially after last summer."

"What about last summer?"

"You know, Janice Allen."

When I still looked blank, he said: "I thought everybody would have known—it was in all the papers."

"I've been abroad."

"Oh, I see. Well, poor little Janice—same age as our Lesley, same class in school—in fact, they were joint dux of the junior school a couple of years ago. Anyway Janice went missing one night. They found her next day in a clump of bushes on the golf course. Stark naked. And strangled."

"Did they get the man?"

"Did they, hell! They're a useless ruddy lot, the police. . . . By God, if I laid hands on the bastard, I know what I'd do to him!"

Shelagh Carey accepted my invitation to dinner, rather to my surprise. I took her to the Prince Regent Hotel.

I hadn't known when I reserved a table that they ran a dinner dance every Saturday night. It was crowded and noisy, and we had to compete with the band to make ourselves heard. But Shelagh didn't seem to mind.

She was wearing a trouser suit—I suppose you'd call it flame-coloured. Anyway, with those big eyes and the glossy, shoulder-length black hair she was a knockout. Even the scar across her cheek gave added allure.

We talked about her school. John Armitage had told me Shelagh was highly regarded as a teacher, and I could well believe it. Her enthusiasm shone through.

But she frowned when I asked about Tom Baines.

"He teaches history," she said.

"He called at my surgery the other night."

"So he told me." Her voice was curt.

"You don't like him?"

"I'm sorry, Mark, if he's a friend of yours, but we're oil and water, Tom and I."

"He's no friend of mine."

"Good. He was a friend of Terry's, and I didn't approve."

"He was at that dinner party, wasn't he, the night Terry was killed?"

"Yes. But please, Mark, don't let's talk about Tom."

The waiters were overworked and the service was slow. We had a long wait between the soup and the fish.

I asked Shelagh to dance.

The tables were ranged round the walls of the dining-room, leaving a central area clear for dancing. About half-a-dozen couples, mostly middle-aged, were on the floor.

It was a waltz and it was at once apparent that Shelagh was a natural on the dance floor: she floated.

After a minute or so she looked up and said: "I'm not made of porcelain, Mark—I won't break."

"What? Oh, I see." I held her more firmly, drew her closer. "That's better!"

So it was. A lot better.

When we got back to the table, she said: "You're not bad, but you don't dance as well as Terry."

"He had more practice."

She looked at me thoughtfully. "Yes, I dare say he had. . . . What's the matter, Mark?"

"Matter?"

"You look upset."

But the waiter appeared with the burgundy I'd ordered. By the time he'd gone I was in control.

It was the perfume—the same perfume Zelda had used. That set the scene. And the first touch of my hand on her bare shoulder did the rest—stirred the aching memory of the whole wretched affair.

I said briskly: "Shelagh, there's a girl in your school called Lesley Peterson. Do you know her?"

She was still watching me with puzzled eyes. But she answered my question. "Yes, she's in my section for English in second year. Very promising girl. Why?"

"I'd like to meet her."

It was unfortunate Lesley hadn't been at home when I called on her father; and I couldn't find a plausible excuse for going back. I thought Shelagh might arrange something.

I explained why I wanted to see Lesley.

Shelagh said: "I do wish you'd drop this, Mark. It's doing no good."

"I thought I'd convinced you. . . . Please help me, Shelagh!"

She sipped her wine while she thought about it. Then she capitulated. "You can come and see me at school on Wednesday after four. I'll find some pretext for keeping Lesley late. That do?"

"You're a pet."

She grinned. "This is why you asked me here, isn't it?"

"Only partly."

"Ah well, the band's good."

I said: "Did you also know Janice Allen?"

The smile disappeared. "You've heard about that, have you?"

"Only this morning. And no details. What happened?"

She told me the story.

"What sort of child was Janice?" I asked, when she'd finished.

"Also very clever. She and Lesley were neck and neck in most subjects. . . . Actually I gave her a lift to the beach that night—I met her by chance in the town."

"She didn't say anything about meeting someone afterwards, I suppose?"

"No, I'm sure she wasn't expecting to. Not at that time of night."

"Were there any rumours about who had done it?"

"I never heard any." But she spoke too quickly.

"What about Terry? He wasn't suspected, was he?" It was a shot in the dark, but it would explain such a lot.

Shelagh said reluctantly: "He was out on the golf course with the Armitages' dog that night. The police put him through the mill. But they let him go. I just don't believe it was Terry."

"Shelagh, I'm *certain* it wasn't Terry." He was incapable of hurting a child, far less killing one.

She nodded. "I'm sure you're right. But the police still suspected him, though they hadn't enough evidence to bring a charge. They think maybe that's why he killed himself—it was on his conscience."

I could see it all now. And not only the police believed it, other people did, too—Armitage and Radford and Baines to my knowledge; and even Shelagh, for all her denials, clearly had her suspicions.

I was very angry.

Shelagh said: "But, Mark, even if Terry had nothing to do with Janice's death, I still think he took his own life. He was terribly depressed, I assure you."

Depressed? Or worried? Mandy had said he was *worried*.

About what? In his letter he'd written: "One night . . . I saw something, innocent in itself, but if you relate it to what happened earlier . . . it's too horrible, it *must* be false . . . I nearly questioned the girl. . . ." Also he'd linked it to something he saw last July. And Janice was murdered in July.

I said: "Shelagh, suppose Terry had stumbled on the identity of the real killer?"

"He'd have gone to the police."

"But if he wasn't sure . . . and especially if it was someone he *knew*. . . ."

"He'd still have gone to the police."

"Not Terry. You know how indecisive he was. He'd brood about it and do nothing—apart from writing to me."

"You're suggesting this might provide a motive for murdering him?"

"Yes."

Shelagh shivered. "I don't believe it," she muttered.

She looked so unhappy that I asked her to dance again.

It was better this time. She was just a girl, not Zelda reincarnated. Come to that, she was a much nicer girl than Zelda, softer, warmer, less self-centered.

Afterwards we talked about the Armitages. Shelagh didn't like them much—not any of them, though she was sorry for Gwen.

"She's had a tough time with these two girls. The younger one in my opinion ought to have remedial teaching. But her mother won't hear of it, and she puts up with *anything* for the sake of peace—Celia just takes advantage, of course. As for John, he keeps out of it: as long as he gets his television in the evenings and his golf at the weekend, he's content."

"And Mandy?"

"Ah yes, Mandy. Nothing wrong with her mental equipment."

"But?"

Shelagh smiled. "There isn't a 'but,' really. I ought to be sorry for her, too. There was some kind of Romeo-Juliet drama when she was about seventeen—you know, first love, disapproving parents, pressure too great for Romeo, Juliet heart-broken. We've all suffered it, haven't we?"

"Yes," I agreed. Some of us when we were much older than seventeen.

She looked quickly at me. "Oh, I know I sound callous, Mark, but *really!* To retire from the world into good works at the age of seventeen—no, I'm sorry, I just can't approve of it."

"I'm sure you're right."

"Now you see how bitchy I am. The goody-goodies always bring out the worst in me."

"I think she's a bit mixed-up," I said.

"Yes, I suppose so. Certainly she's had precious little love from her father or her stepmother. Gwen's jealous of her."

"Jealous?"

"Yes. Of her looks. And her youth, I suppose."

"Her *looks?*"

"Oh yes, Mandy Armitage could put Gwen in the shade if she wanted to. Come to that, she could put *me* in the shade."

"That's nonsense."

"It's not, you know. But she deliberately *chooses* to look a frump. A form of masochism. I tell you, a psychiatrist could have himself a ball in that household. Terry and I used to discuss them by the hour."

"Why did Terry stay there? It must have been hell for someone like him."

She suddenly closed up. "He had his reasons," she said abruptly.

When I delivered Shelagh to her flat at half-past ten, I declined her invitation to go in for a drink. I didn't want to start anything. Not yet, anyway.

Besides, I had another call to make tonight. I'd been thinking about Lesley Peterson, worrying about her. If she knew something, she might be in danger, too. She was the same age as Janice Allen, she might be in the same *kind* of danger. My appointment with her next Wednesday was a long way off.

I drove to the police station. I said to the man at the desk: "I don't suppose Detective Inspector Robens will be here at this hour, but—"

A voice from the back interrupted me. "Why should you suppose that? Twenty-four hours a day, seven days a week—that's me."

He took me into the C.I.D. room. "I was going to ring you

tomorrow," he said. "We've failed to trace your anonymous correspondent. Frankly, it's what I expected."

Frankly, it was what I'd expected, too.

So I told him now about Lesley Peterson. It's difficult to be convincing when your audience is openly sceptical, and I told the story badly.

Robens said: "I don't understand, Dr. Kendall. You say this girl may be in danger. Why?"

"Because of something that happened a week or two before my brother's death." I explained again, but he remained unimpressed.

"You're making bricks without straw," he said.

"At least you can question the girl."

"What about?"

"About what happened that night. September 14, it was."

"You think it has some bearing on your brother's death?"

"It could have. *And* Janice Allen's."

"Ah!" He nodded as if he understood at last. "I see. Well, that clears the air a bit. I didn't mean to bring this up, I wanted to spare you, but now I must tell you. The Janice Allen case is closed, her killer is dead."

"You mean Terry?"

"Yes. . . . Now, just a minute—" as I tried to interrupt. "Listen to the facts. Your brother had psychiatric treatment a few years ago. Right?"

"Yes, but—"

"Secondly, he was in the habit of meeting girls—or a girl—on the golf course late at night for purposes of fornication. That is established fact, Dr. Kendall."

"I don't doubt it. But were these girls thirteen years old?"

He waved a hand to concede the point. "According to the descriptions we've had, they were a bit older. But nevertheless *girls*. And note where these encounters took place: in a shed not thirty yards from where Janice's body was found. . . . Finally, the three girls who cycled home saw him crossing the golf course with the dog towards the stile that Janice would go over. He *must* have seen her, yet he denied it. What do you say to that, Doctor?"

"The girl wasn't raped, as I understand it?"

"No. Our guess is she struggled, screamed perhaps. He panicked, compressed her throat to shut her up, then found he had a corpse on his hands. It happens."

"Terry could charm the pants off a girl any time he wanted. He'd never use force. And anyway thirteen-year-olds weren't in his line."

The inspector was unconvinced. "He was scared as a rabbit when we questioned him," he said.

"Yes, he would be. He was no hero, Terry. But equally he was no murderer."

Robens shrugged. "We hadn't enough evidence for a conviction, so we let him go. But we kept tabs on him. And he acted like a man with a load on his mind."

"All the time? Right back from July?"

"He was much worse latterly," he conceded. "It must have been building up. It was no surprise to me when his body was found at the foot of the cliffs. What do you say to that, Doctor?"

It seemed to be a favourite conversational gambit. "I say you ought to talk to Lesley Peterson."

He snorted in disgust. "I'll think about it," he said.

PROLOGUE TO PART III

When I grow up, Lesley Peterson reflected, I'm going to study *all* the religions—Mohammedanism, Buddhism, the lot. Just because you happened to be born in England, why should Anglicans be right and everyone else wrong?

She often had these rebellious thoughts on a Sunday after an hour in church listening to the Reverend Tyfield and then nearly another hour here in Sunday school. Anne Ridley was lucky: her parents were freethinkers or something and Anne never had to go to church at all.

Still, as Sunday-school teachers went, Mandy Armitage, who took the twelve- and thirteen-year-olds, wasn't bad. A bit square, but quite nice really. She'd been very friendly with Lesley's brother Kenny at one time, but that was years ago, before Kenny went to university.

They'd been hearing about St. Paul's travels today, and it was fascinating to trace them on that big map Mandy had brought along. Of course, as usual Celia Armitage did her best to wreck the lesson, interrupting her stepsister with stupid questions and generally making a nuisance of herself. One had to make allowances, but in Lesley's view, even if you weren't very bright, you didn't have to be *nasty*.

Although the same age as herself, Celia was still in the junior school; so it was only on a Sunday they came together. That was more than enough. When Sunday school broke up, Lesley always nipped out quickly to try to escape Celia. It seldom worked.

It didn't today: Celia caught up with her.

She said: "My daddy says your daddy needs his tummy taken out. If he doesn't, he'll die." And when Lesley didn't answer, she added: "Maybe he'll die anyway."

"Shut up!"

Celia giggled. It was always a mistake to let her see she'd drawn blood.

Celia said: "I know who killed Jan Allen."

A shiver ran down Lesley's spine. She still had nightmares about that experience last month, when she thought she was going to suffer the same fate as Janice.

"Don't be silly!" she said. "How could you know?"

"Uncle Ben told me."

"Who's Uncle Ben?"

"Dr. Radford, of course. . . . You'll never guess who it was that killed Janice."

That was the trouble, she *could* guess. . . .

"Who?" she said.

"Dr. Kendall!"

Lesley laughed with relief. Trust Celia to come out with something nutty.

"It's true! Uncle Ben said he killed Janice and then he threw himself over the cliff cause he was going to be found out. So there!"

"That's rot!" But she wasn't laughing now. Suppose she'd got things upside down: suppose it was *Dr. Kendall* she should have been scared of. Come to think of it, it was queer the way he was always walking with that dog on the golf course, even after dark. And both times she'd seen him after that night—when he called to see her father next day, and when she'd gone to the surgery for prescriptions—both times he'd looked at her in a funny sort of way. Maybe he was mad.

She didn't want to believe it. Dr. Kendall had been one of her heroes, she'd woven romantic dreams round him. He was so handsome—like that picture of Lord Byron in her poetry book. Much nicer-looking than his brother, the new Dr. Kendall: *he* looked so stuffy!

No, she wouldn't believe it. "Dr. Kendall didn't throw himself over the cliff," she said witheringly. "It was an accident. It said so in the paper."

"That's all *you* know," Celia sneered, and ran off.

When Lesley got home, her mother said: "There's someone to see you. He's in the sitting-room."

"Who?"

"Inspector Robens. . . . He wants to ask you a few more questions. Shall I go in with you?"

"Oh no, Mother, it's all right."

The inspector was standing at the window, reading the *News of the World*. He looked such a sad man, Lesley always thought. He'd lost a little girl from polio a year or two ago. Lesley still remembered the hearse passing, with the tiny little coffin. It brought a lump to her throat.

The inspector laid down his paper. "Come and sit down, Lesley. This won't take long."

If it was about that night last July, she'd nothing more to tell him. She'd gone swimming with Anne and Janice and Pat at Abbot's Creek. Janice hadn't her bike with her, because it had a puncture, so the other three left her to walk home. They'd all been worried about how late they were and thought of nothing but getting home as quickly as possible to avoid a row. Of course, if they'd ever imagined Jan would be in any *danger*. . . .

They all saw Dr. Kendall up on the golf course with his dog, walking down towards the stile. . . . Heavens! she'd never seen the significance of *that* before. It hadn't crossed her mind anyone might suspect Dr. Kendall.

However, it wasn't about Janice the inspector was asking today. "Lesley, do you remember the evening of September 14?"

"Goodness, that's over a month ago, Mr. Robens." She managed to keep her voice steady.

"It was the day your school went back. And I believe your father took ill at the clubhouse—"

"Oh yes, I remember."

"What did you do after school that day?"

She wrinkled her brow, pretending to concentrate. "I think I— yes, I'm sure of it. I went to Anne Ridley's for tea. She's my friend."

"And then?"

"I came home."

"Straight home?"

"Yes." There, the lie wasn't so difficult!

"At what time?"

"It was just getting dark. About half-past eight."

"Did anything unusual happen on your way home—or at any other time that night?"

"What sort of thing, Mr. Robens?"

"I don't know. I'm asking you, Lesley."

"No, nothing at all. I just walked home, and there was Daddy ill and Mother in a flap." Gosh! what if he asked to see her diary!

The inspector hesitated, then he said: "Perhaps I should be more specific. Did you see Dr. Kendall—the *late* Dr. Kendall—at any time that evening?"

Ah! she'd been right! They were out to blacken his name. You'd think they'd stop hounding a man after he was dead. She was glad now she'd told those lies.

"Dr. Kendall? No, I'm sure I didn't. Of course, he could have passed in his car without me seeing him."

Detective Inspector Robens stood up. "You've been very helpful, Lesley," he said.

"I don't understand what it was all about."

He smiled. "I was acting, as they say, on information received. And as so often is the case, it was *false*."

Afterwards Lesley went over in her mind what *really* happened that night the inspector was talking about. It was the first day back at school after the summer holidays, and she'd gone straight from school to Anne Ridley's for tea.

Her mother had warned her she must be home before dark. But she stayed at Anne's too long, and the light was already fading when she set off home. Never mind, if she hurried she'd make it in time to avoid a rocket.

But, as always, Lesley was drawn, like a moth to a flame, to Kingsley's lighted window in High Street. She loved bookshops and dreamed of the day when she would own stacks and stacks of books.

Tonight her eyes feasted on the fat, leather-bound volume in the centre of the window: *The Complete Works of William Shake-speare*. Gosh! All in one book! What must that cost?

Another, larger, reflection appeared beside her own in the window and a voice said: "It's Lesley, isn't it?"

Startled, Lesley look round, then smiled. "I didn't hear you coming," she said.

"Isn't it rather late for a little girl to be out on her own?"

"I'm thirteen and a bit." She was cross. Why did she have to be so *small?* Why should Anne Ridley be three inches taller although she was six weeks younger? It wasn't fair.

"All the same it's getting dark. . . ."

"I'm on my way home."

"I'll give you a lift."

Never talk to strangers; above all, never accept a lift from strangers. How often had her parents repeated the warning? Especially since that ghastly business about Jan last summer.

But this wasn't a stranger. "Thanks, that would be super," Lesley said, and got in.

The car was warm, and there was a piece of chocolate for her. What a groovy way to end the day!

Soon Lesley was chattering happily. Her mother was always saying she talked too much, her tongue would trip her one of these days. But you could tell she didn't *really* mind.

Suddenly Lesley became conscious of the prolonged whine of low gear. She looked out and saw the lights of the town winking far below her.

"This is the wrong way!" she said. "I live on Blaikie Street!"

"It's all right, Lesley, I've a call to make at the golf clubhouse. It won't take five minutes, then I'll run you home."

Lesley was silent now as the car continued to climb. She wasn't alarmed exactly, but puzzled. Surely it would have been more sensible to drop her at Blaikie Street first?

Presently the driver muttered an imprecation and the car slowed.

"What's the matter?" Lesley said.

"I've taken the wrong fork."

Lesley looked out. The golf clubhouse was fifty yards on their left, all lit up, and the strains of music from a television set filtered out. Her father would be in there with his friends, she reflected, and wondered if she should shout. But he wouldn't hear, nobody would hear; and anyway she'd look an awful *fool*.

They had branched off the main road to the clubhouse and were on a narrow lane between hedges. Lesley considered opening the door and jumping out, but the car had picked up speed again. "No room to turn," the driver explained. "We'll need to go to the end."

About half a mile further on the surface of the road deteriorated and the headlights showed that it petered out into a footpath rising up towards the cliffs.

The car swung in a half circle and parked on short grass. The lights picked out a white flag flapping on a post: this must still be part of the golf course. In the distance the green light of a plane descended towards the airfield.

The engine of the car was shut off and the headlights extinguished. It was almost dark. Lesley sensed rather than saw the movement beside her.

She said very clearly: "Oh look! There's Bess!"

"What?" The movement was arrested.

"The dog. And Dr. Kendall." She wound down the window. "Bess! Bess! Here, Bess! Hullo, Dr. Kendall!" she shouted.

He was some distance away, but she'd spotted him just before the headlights went out. She wasn't sure if he'd heard, but the dog ran towards the car, then stood barking and wagging its tail.

The driver exclaimed: "Goodness, look at the time, Lesley! You should be home in bed."

The engine was switched on, they reversed in a rapid arc, then roared away. They drove on backlights until they rejoined the main road.

"Thank you for the lift," Lesley said formally as she got out at Blaikie Street.

"A pleasure. Don't tell your parents it was my fault you were late."

"No, of course not."

All the same, she would have told if her mother had given her the expected rocket. But she returned to a domestic crisis. Her father's ulcer had acted up again and he'd had to be brought home from the golf clubhouse. Her mother was trying to get a doctor and didn't even notice how late Lesley was.

In the cold light of morning Lesley decided she had panicked for no reason: it had all been perfectly innocent. She blushed to think of the terrible accusations she'd so nearly blurted out. Even so, she almost mentioned the incident to Dr. Kendall when he called to see her father next morning; but she didn't.

There was one person, though, she wouldn't be accepting a lift from again.

That had happened a month ago and Lesley hadn't yet lost entirely the sense of shock and fear the experience had produced. But she'd never before thought of *Dr. Kendall* as the potential villain of the piece.

Yet what had he been doing there at that hour? Just as he'd been hanging around the night Janice was murdered. Maybe it was lucky the driver had nipped away so smartly when Dr. Kendall appeared. Otherwise they might both have had their chips.

She didn't really believe Dr. Kendall was a murderer. But even if he was, he was dead now, so what good could it do to rake over the past? She was glad she hadn't told the inspector anything about the incident.

Next to Saturday, Monday was Lesley's favourite day of the week. A super day at school: two periods of English as well as French and gym; while the afternoon timetable included singing, which was a riot. And there was still the evening to look forward to.

Today started with a bang. Miss Carey announced the casting for the play-reading the class was going to do for the Christmas concert. It was scenes from *The Merchant of Venice,* and Lesley was given the role of Portia. Gosh! the star part! She felt her face go scarlet with excitement: she couldn't wait to get home to tell her parents.

As they were leaving the English classroom, Miss Carey called her back. "Lesley, that last essay of yours—there were one or two points I wanted to discuss with you."

"Oh yes, Miss Carey?"

"I wondered if you'd come round here at four o'clock on Wednesday. It won't take more than a few minutes."

"Oh *yes,* Miss Carey." If Miss Carey had asked her to jump off a cliff, she'd have said "Oh *yes,* Miss Carey."

"Run along, then."

For the rest of the day Lesley trod on air. At break she recorded the news in her diary. If you kept a diary, you had to write things down while the mood was fresh. And as soon as she was home from school at four, she got her *Merchant of Venice* out to study her lines. Gosh! wasn't it a big part! And some real groovy bits: "The quality of mercy is not strain'd, it droppeth as the gentle rain from heaven . . ."

For once she was almost sorry when Anne and Elma called for her at six o'clock. The Monday-night visit to the cinema was now an established ritual. Elma, Anne's sister, who was eighteen, was receptionist at the Lion and was on duty till eight o'clock each night except Mondays and Saturdays. On Saturdays she went out with her boy friend, on Mondays she chaperoned Anne and Lesley. It was a condition on which Lesley's parents insisted when she went out on winter nights: someone older had to call for her and bring her home.

What her mother and father *didn't* know was that George, the boy friend, accompanied them; and that for the last four or five weeks he'd whisked Elma off on his motor bike as soon as they came out of the cinema, leaving the two younger girls to find their own way home.

Although unhappy about the deception, Lesley didn't dare give away the secret in case it broke up her friendship with Anne. That would be dreadful! Anyway, it was only ten minutes' walk from the cinema to Blaikie Street. Anne had *miles* further to go.

Tonight George was waiting outside the cinema, as usual. He gave Elma a juicy kiss, smacked Lesley on the bottom and said: "When are you going to grow some beef, kid?" Right there in the street, with people watching!

But he was nice. He always gave Anne and Lesley money to buy sweets with, though they usually saved it for chips afterwards.

Once inside they separated, George and Elma going for the back row if they could. Anne and Lesley went well forward: Anne's sight wasn't too good and she refused to wear her glasses.

The main film tonight was a musical, one of these big technicolor spectaculars. Lesley found it a bit boring and her thoughts wandered. She'd decided she was going to be an actress. . . .

When they came out, the only trace of George and Elma was the sound of a motorcycle exhaust disappearing down High Street. The two girls walked round to Francini's Fish Grill.

They bought chips and stood on the pavement outside, eating them. Anne was raving about the film. She hadn't very good *taste*, Lesley reflected, in things like films and books; and as for poetry, she thought it was one big yawn.

But that was why they got on so well: they complemented each other. There was no rivalry, as there had been with Janice. Anne was a wow at subjects like math and arithmetic and science—she could even beat her father at chess! And Lesley scored in the arty subjects. It was a perfect balance. The only cloud in the sky was Anne's growing interest in boys. It would be a *disaster* if she got a boy friend and ditched Lesley.

Anne said: "Did you see Dr. Radford in the flicks?"

"No."

"He was just behind us."

It was always a worry in case someone saw them and mentioned to Lesley's mother or father that Elma hadn't been with them. A week or two before they'd bumped into Miss Carey. Not that *she* was likely to pass it on. Or Dr. Radford either, for that matter. But you could never be sure.

That stink, Celia Armitage, had somehow found out as well. She'd mentioned it to Lesley on the way home from school the other day. *She* was the type to spill the beans if she knew they weren't supposed to be out alone.

" 'Oh, what a tangled web we weave . . .' " Lesley quoted.

"What?"

"Poetry."

Anne groaned.

The clock on St. Saviour's tower began to strike.

"Gosh!" Lesley said. "It can't be!"

But it was. It was ten o'clock.

"I'll need to *fly*, or they'll have a search party out." And that would be the end of the Monday evenings.

Lesley was already dashing up Piper Lane. She knew she ought to go the long way round. But she never did: the short cut saved a full two minutes.

Piper Lane was a narrow, ill-lit alley connecting Woodstock Road with High Street. McKenzie's warehouse extended most of the way down the east side, while on the other side were slum properties, mostly derelict and condemned, although a few were still occupied.

It was a one-way street—indeed, there was no room for two cars to pass. Not that cars used Piper Lane much: there were easier ways of proceeding from Woodstock Road to High Street.

There was a car there tonight, though, parked without lights, its offside wheels on the pavement. Lesley barely noticed it as she ran uphill towards the lights of High Street. But as she drew alongside, the driver's door suddenly jerked open and she ran straight into it.

She gasped with pain and shock and turned to protest. The driver was already half out of the car and in the courtesy light from the interior she saw who it was. She opened her mouth to scream, but no sound came, for hands were on her neck, compressing her throat. Then she was being dragged, barely conscious, into the car. The door slammed shut.

PART III

CELIA ARMITAGE

CHAPTER I

They all say I'm stupid. Well, maybe I'm no good at sums and grammar and all that rot. But I'm not so dumb as they think.

One of the first things I remember is Daddy saying: "But the child's not *normal*, Gwen."

And Mummy screeched: "Don't you dare say that!" They were always going on at each other about me. Mummy fussed over me and Daddy tried to pretend I wasn't there.

He was ashamed of me—still is. He told me once I was the cause of his asthma.

Oh, he hides it well, never shows it. But I'm a great big disappointment to him, even worse than Mandy. He'd like to forget about me, he hates meeting other girls my age.

And Mummy? Well, she puts a face on it, pretends there's nothing wrong. In a way that's worse, because deep down she doesn't really believe it, and she's bitter as hell. ("Watch your language, Celia!" I can hear Mandy say. Why shouldn't I swear? *She* swears sometimes.)

You see, I understand all this. I'm thirteen and I'm two classes behind at school and I'm slow. But I didn't *go* to school till I was seven. And I do understand things. They needn't treat me like Bess, the dog: I'm there and I'm listening and I'm taking it in. It *pays* to act stupid.

And it pays to act tough, too. If you don't look after yourself, no one else will. Most people hate scenes: I get a kick out of them and it gets me my own way.

I don't care whether people like me or not. I know they won't anyway. Nobody's ever liked me—well, except one, Uncle Ben, I mean. No one else.

Not even Mummy. She does her best, but she doesn't really *enjoy* being with me. And Mandy feels sorry for me and that makes me wild. . . .

I hate the lot of them. They want me to behave like other children. But, as Uncle Ben says, why shouldn't I be myself? We can't all be swots like Jan Allen or Lesley Peterson. And see what happened to them. It makes me feel great to think of that. I hated them, they were a couple of stinking snobs, both of them.

Mummy used to make a fuss of them—that whole crowd, Anne Ridley and Pat Richards as well. She tried to get me accepted. What a hope! Stinking, stinking snobs, every one, except maybe Anne, she's not quite so rotten.

Daddy hated it, he knew they turned up their noses at me. And so did their parents. They never invited me back. Well, I was at Jan's once or twice, but I could see her mother didn't really approve.

The mothers were scared of me, I was supposed to be "vicious." Lesley actually told me that once. So I twisted her arm, just for the hell of it. If that's what they thought of me, I'd show them.

I've always been big for my age, and very strong—stronger than any of them. The other girls used to laugh at me when I said something stupid in class. Or when I wet my pants. Very funny, ha ha!

Until I belted a girl one day and loosened two teeth. What a fuss there was! The headmistress was up seeing Mummy, there was talk about sending me to a special school. But it all blew over.

Nobody ever laughed at me again.

I saw Jan Allen the night she was murdered. She was with the usual crowd down at the creek—it was a hot night and they were going for a swim.

I was horsing around with Helen Potts—not really hurting her, just fooling—when Jan came up and *ordered* me to let her go. I got such a surprise I loosened my grip and Helen wriggled away (I soon caught her again, of course).

Usually Jan was scared stiff of me, they all were, but I suppose she felt safe because there were four of them. I didn't take them on, I just marked Jan down for later. Next day when I heard that somebody had done her in, I laughed like a drain. . . .

Stupid fool to let anyone do that to her! Served her right. I'd like to see any man try it with me—I know exactly where I'd kick him.

I don't like men anyway. Or boys. I saw Anne Ridley yesterday hand in hand with that spotty boy Fredericks. Ugh!

Mandy says I'll change, I'll come to like boys, but she's talking rot.

Fat lot of good boys have done Mandy. She was potty over that Kenny Peterson, the one that's grown a beard now, and he chucked her. Then she fell for Dr. Kendall and he chucked her, too. It's a laugh when you think of it.

Actually Terry Kendall wasn't too bad, not like that stink of a brother of his. He treated me like I was human and let me call him Terry. (I just can't *imagine* calling the new Dr. Kendall "Mark"!) Sometimes he would read my comic to me after I was in bed. Even Mummy won't do that.

But latterly Terry went all broody and miserable and he'd no time for me. I heard Dr. Cohen tell Daddy they'd have to get rid of him and I wondered what he'd done wrong. So I asked Uncle Ben.

Uncle Ben's the only person I can really *talk* to. It's always been like that. I mean, he doesn't try to change me the way the others do—like "Do you never read anything but these silly comics?" or "You might at least keep yourself *clean*, Celia." No, Uncle Ben doesn't bother about all that rot, he's just interested in *me*. I wish he was my daddy.

So I asked him about Terry.

"Well, pet," he said (he's always called me "pet"), "people are talking."

"How do you mean, *talking?*"

"About the man who murdered your friend Janice."

"She wasn't my friend, Uncle Ben. She was a stinking snob."

"Well, anyway, there's a rumour going round it was Dr. Kendall. . . ."

Gosh! I'd often wondered who it was, of course. I thought it might be Peeping Tom, he has a dirty mind, he's always trying to see up our dresses. But Terry! Gosh, think of the times I'd been alone with him in my bedroom at night! What if he'd . . . I got a funny tingling feeling all up and down my back.

"Of course, it's a damned lie," Uncle Ben said.

The tingling stopped. "What's going to happen, then?" I asked. "Will they sack him?"

"Not while I'm here, pet, not while I'm here." He was terrific, Uncle Ben—so calm always and so strong. I said that to Mandy once and she laughed. I could have killed her.

Well, they didn't sack Terry. They didn't need to, because just a night or two after that he fell over the cliff and got himself killed. His head was smashed like an eggshell, and a girl I know said they found splashes of blood half a mile away!

Uncle Ben told me he'd thrown himself over the cliff, so it must have been him after all that murdered Jan. But nobody else seemed to know this, only Uncle Ben.

Terry's brother came for the funeral. I didn't meet him the first night, I was in bed feeling lousy. But a day or two later he moved into our house and took Terry's old room.

A proper stink he was. Looked at you as if you weren't there. Funny thing was, Mandy loathed him, too; she was even ruder to him than I was.

Uncle Ben says Mandy and I really have a lot in common. I don't see it. Mandy's clever and she works like stink and she tries to help people. Me, I don't help people.

Take Sunday school. Mandy teaches in Sunday school and I go because it passes the time and Sunday morning's dead anyway. But I don't believe all that crap about God that she yaks about.

Mandy's dead serious about it. So I get a kick out of asking stupid questions, seeing how far I can go. It gets her worried. She's never sure whether I'm being cheeky or not.

Funny thing, though—sometimes I feel rotten about it. I mean, Mandy's dead straight, she'd never do you a dirty trick. But I tell myself, that's just being soppy, and anyway where did straightness ever get Mandy?

Of course, the real fun came from baiting Lesley Peterson. It was the only chance I got, because she was two classes above me at school and she would pass me in the playground with her nose in the air as if I was dirt. To think that Mummy wanted me to be friends with that pig! The day I twisted her arm—when she told me her mother thought I was "vicious"—I nearly broke it, I was so mad.

She told on me, of course, and I got a jawing from the rector. Any more trouble and I'd be out, he said. So I never touched her in school again.

I made up for it on Sundays, interrupted when she was trying to suck up to Mandy, tormented the life out of her on the way home. I don't know why she kept coming. Yes, I do, it was because she was a stinking swot and liked to show off.

On the way home last Sunday, I don't remember how it came up, but I told her what Uncle Ben had said—you know, that it was Terry Kendall who'd murdered Jan Allen and then killed himself. I knew that would make her mad, because he was Lesley's doctor and she thought he was groovy. Anything Lesley had was perfect.

Well, you should have seen her face! She looked like she was going to have kittens.

"It couldn't *possibly* have been Dr. Kendall," she said.

"How do you know?"

"Because—oh why should I bother telling *you?*" And suddenly she darted off up the road.

I let her go. It was queer, she'd sounded as if she really *did* know something.

I told Uncle Ben. He didn't think much of it. "Just showing off," he said. "Pretending she knows more than she does. Everyone tries it. *You* often do, pet."

Yes, but that was different. I told lies whenever it suited me, nobody ever believed me anyway. Lesley wasn't like me—or so everybody said.

Well, what did it matter? So she knew something I didn't. Who cared? She was just a stinking swot.

Although I'm still in the junior school, when I get fed up with Helen Potts and Freda Landy I stroll around the senior cloakroom at break until I get chucked out. I like to keep tabs on what they're doing and saying.

On Monday I found Lesley sitting in the cloakroom writing up her diary.

For years she'd kept a diary in a school exercise book. Every ruddy thing went down. I'd pinched it once and read it—it was sick-making: "Miss C. gave me V.G. for essay!!! Jan only got G+ . . ." That sort of guff.

Today she looked up as I passed and quickly covered up what she was writing. As if I cared . . .

I said: "Who do you think's going to read that crap, Lesley?"

She closed the book.

"I mean, it's such rot, isn't it? 'Got up, brushed my teeth, sat on the loo . . .'"

She turned red. "It's not like that at all."

"Well, what, then?"

"It's none of your business and you shouldn't be hanging around here, anyway," she said in that snooty voice, stuffing the diary into her school-bag.

That made me mad. Well, I mean, it was the *way* she said it, like I was dirt. Just because she was a swot and was two classes above me. I'd have loved to smash her face in.

But I had a better idea. Lesley's form gets gym first period on a Monday afternoon, while we're having Peeping Tom for history. Half-way through the lesson I put my hand up and asked to be excused.

Baines looked as if he was going to be rude about it but all he said was: "Well, we'd better let you go, hadn't we?"

Titters from the class, but they soon stopped when I glared at them.

As soon as I was outside, I ran across to the gym, then crept up the stairs into the changing room. I could hear the floor of the gym thumping as they did one of these stupid exercises.

The school-bags were scattered round the changing room beside the clothes they'd taken off. I soon found Lesley's. It was crammed with text books and exercise books and I'd a job finding the diary. Just to make it harder she'd marked it "English Literature" on the outside.

I took it to the loo and was just going to drop it down the W.C. when I thought I might as well *read* it first, so I stuffed it under my clothes and went back to my classroom.

Old Baines said: "Welcome back, Miss Armitage," but he didn't seem to notice the bulge.

While he was yakking on, I slipped the exercise book out from under my jersey and shoved it in my own bag.

Coming out at four, I caught up with Lesley and Anne Ridley. They were always together, these two, especially since Jan died. Sometimes Pat Richards was with them as well.

"Going to the pictures tonight?" I said.

Anne said, "Yes." Lesley walked on with her head in the air.

"Who's taking you home, Lesley?"

I knew this would make her mad. She came home alone and her mother didn't know that. I'd found out weeks ago, and she was scared I'd tell.

"Why can't you leave me *alone?*" she said, nearly blubbing. But she never mentioned the diary, she couldn't have missed it yet.

I took out the diary as soon as I got home. It started on July 1 and filled most of the exercise book, a day to each page. Every one ended "And so to bed."

I looked to see what she'd been writing at break this morning. It was just a few lines: "Wonderful, *wonderful* news this morning. Miss C. has chosen me as Portia for the play-reading! . . . More later after the flicks."

Portia? Who the hell was Portia?

I flicked back over the pages, but it was all the same sort of crap. She *was* a prize wet.

One page looked different from the rest. September 14 it was, that's five weeks ago. It began in the usual soppy way: "Writing this at break. Super to be back at school, though the others groan. Even Peeping Tom seems tolerable after two months' absence. Miss C. for English again—hooray! More later."

But the rest of the page was crammed with such tiny writing I could hardly make it out. I'd just read "Big adventure tonight . . ." when the door opened and Mandy came in. I shut the book.

"Well, well," she said. "What goes?"

"I've been doing my homework."

She laughed. "That'll be the day."

I put the diary in my school-bag and closed the bag. I said: "Bet you don't know who Dr. Kendall had dinner with Saturday night."

"No, and I'm not interested." Mandy was still very snooty to the new Dr. Kendall, but I just had a *feeling* she wouldn't like to hear this all the same.

"Well, it was Miss Carey." It had been all round school today: someone had seen them at the Prince Regent on Saturday. "They were dancing, too," I said. "Cheek to cheek. Square!"

"How nice for Miss Carey," Mandy said. Yes, I'd been right: she didn't look too chuffed about it. Of course, Miss Carey had grabbed the *other* Dr. Kendall from her.

Mandy was going out when she turned around and said: "Celia, what makes you tick?"

"My heart." She asked me that before.

"I mean, what are we doing wrong? Do you not get enough love, is that it?"

Whenever anyone mentions love to me, I want to throw up. You can't get anywhere on love, you have to use your teeth and claws.

"I get enough," I said.

CHAPTER 2

Monday nights I go to the Guides. So I have high tea at half-past five all by myself.

Well, I *eat* it myself, but Mummy's usually there chatting. Asking questions, mostly. "How did you get on at school today? Were you speaking to Pat? Or Lesley? What did they say?"

She's potty about that crowd. I mean, what's so special about them, except they're a lot of swots?

"They're not even in my *class*," I tell her.

"But they're your own *age*, darling. I'm not happy about you going round with young girls like Helen Potts."

"She's not a stink like those other ones."

I don't know why she bothers, because it doesn't make a scrap of difference, I do exactly what I like. She wouldn't dare stop me.

I told her today that Lesley had been rude to me.

She put her lips together that funny way—she hates hearing that sort of thing.

"I hope you didn't give her any cause."

"Of course not."

I scooped out some egg and made Bess beg for it. I loathe boiled eggs.

"Can I go to the pictures tonight?" I said.

"Don't be silly. It's your Guides night."

"I'm fed up with Guides."

But just then Daddy and Dr. Kendall came in. "We've just been coping with an emergency," Daddy said. "Is there any tea going?"

He was breathing in that wheezy way, kidding he had asthma. I'd learned to do that, too, just from watching him. I could take in everybody except Uncle Ben.

Mummy got two more cups from the kitchen and poured the tea for them. She never once looked at Daddy.

It's funny the way they go on, they're like strangers, I mean, they sleep in different rooms and they never go out together, and when they're both home at night Mummy sits in the drawing-room while Daddy's in his study.

Even at meals they hardly ever speak to each other. And that's queer because when Mummy's with anyone else it's yak, yak, yak all the time. After I'm in bed at night I can hear her voice going on and on to Dr. Kendall.

I asked Uncle Ben once: "Why did they bother getting married, was it just for sex or something?" But Uncle Ben doesn't like that sort of talk and told me I was too young to understand.

I said to Daddy: "Mummy won't let me go to the pictures."

"Well, don't bother me. I'm flaked out."

He was always too tired, or too busy, or too worried to have any time for me. All the same he never missed his favourite T.V. programmes—he wasn't too busy for *that*.

I said: "But it's *Funny Girl*. Miss Carey said we should go to it."

Dr. Kendall said: "Tell you what, Celia—I'll take you later in the week."

"Stuff that! I want to go tonight."

He looked like he wanted to hit me, and even Mummy just about broke her jaw trying not to look angry. All she said was: "You're not coming home on your own at that time of night."

"Lesley Peterson goes to the flicks every Monday and *she* comes home on her own."

Mummy said: "You'd think that once bitten, twice shy . . . But even if Lesley sticks her neck out, that's no reason why you should do the same."

Daddy was stuffing himself with cherry cake and I thought he wasn't listening. But he said: "You've got it wrong, anyway, Celia. Harry Peterson told me the older Ridley girl and her sister see Lesley home."

"Ha ha! That's all *he* knows. Lesley goes for chips with Anne and then hoofs it home alone. He doesn't know George goes to the pictures with Elma and they go off on his motor bike."

Lesley would be furious if she knew I'd told them. For, sure as fate, Daddy would pass it on to her old man.

But Daddy just yawned and said: "I've a patient to visit after supper tonight, Gwen. And I might call in at the club afterwards." Even now he didn't look at her. And Mummy didn't answer.

He was still wheezing. Must be for real this time.

When I'd finished my tea, I changed into my Guide uniform. I said to Mummy: "I need a pound."

"What for?"

"Captain said we were to bring it this week."

"But what *for?*"

"Guide camp."

"A deposit, you mean?"

"Yeah, that was the word."

She got out her purse and gave me a pound note. It's a laugh, really, because I bet she *knew* what I wanted it for. But she has to act like she believes I never tell lies.

Mandy tells her she's nutty to let me off with things, and I guess Mandy's right. But why should I worry?

I hurried to catch Helen Potts before she went into the Guide hut. She was scared when I told her.

"But it doesn't come out till half-past nine, Celia. Anyway, I've no money."

"I've enough for us both."

"My mum'll skin me if I'm late home."

I gripped her arm tight, till it hurt. "I'll skin you if you don't come," I said. I can make her do anything.

"Well, O.K.," she squealed after a bit. "I said, *O.K.*"

Sometimes I wonder what it would be like to go on and on till they're screaming for mercy. And *still* not let go.

We got seats in the back row of the stalls, just along from Elma Ridley and her boy friend, George. *They* didn't see much of the film, they were just about glued together.

I didn't see Anne and Lesley, they'd be down near the front because Anne's half blind and won't wear her specs. But I saw Uncle Ben, he seemed to be by himself. I don't think he noticed us.

I got bored with the picture. Too much singing in it, just one big yawn, though Helen was gazing at it with her mouth open like it was wonderful.

I found a pin in the pocket of my Guide tunic and I jabbed it into her backside and she just about hit the roof. I felt better after that.

Afterwards I went into the picture house cafe and had a Coke and two doughnuts. Helen wouldn't come, she was crazy to get home. So I let her go. But I made her go and look to see if Mummy was waiting outside. She wasn't.

I asked for a packet of fags but the girl at the desk wouldn't give me them. I was quite glad really, because they still make me puke. But I *must* get used to them.

It was nearly ten o'clock when I came out. Still no sign of Mummy. So I strolled up High Street. It's great being out alone in the lights and the crowds late at night.

First street you come to after the Regent is Piper Lane, a dark, narrow lane that leads down to Woodstock Road. I looked down as I was passing to see if Anne and Lesley were there. They always go to Francini's after the pictures and stand in Piper Lane to eat their chips because it's dark there and they don't want people to see them.

There *were* two girls, I suppose it was them but it was too dark to be sure.

The St. Saviour's clock began to strike and one of the girls started running up Piper Lane towards me. I think the other one went off down Woodstock Road, but I'm not sure.

There was a car parked in the lane quite near the foot. I hadn't noticed it at first, but just as the girl was running past, the driver opened his door and she went slap into it. She ended up on the pavement on her behind. I laughed like a drain. I hoped it *was* Lesley.

The driver leant out and helped her into the car. That seemed to be it, so I just walked on.

Well, I mean, how was I to *know?* And it was so dark I couldn't *possibly* have recognised the car. Or the driver. Though I had a funny feeling at the time—but that was just stupid. It could have been anyone. I can't think why I felt so sick about it.

I got home at quarter-past ten. Mandy said: "You've had a ball, haven't you? Where have you been?"

"At the Guides."

"Pull the other one. Lucky for you they're both out."

"They wouldn't give me a row anyway, so there!"

"No, that's the sad bit. . . . Did you enjoy the film?"

"Not much."

"Are you all right, Celia?"

"Why?"

"You look as if you'd seen a ghost."

"I'm *fine*." She was too sharp, Mandy.

"All right, hop it. You'd better be in bed when they get back."

Next morning I was having my cornflakes and reading my comic at breakfast while Dr. Kendall stuffed himself on bacon and egg. We never spoke to each other. I heard him telling Dr. Cohen one day that he'd like to tan the hide off me. Just let him try!

Mandy always had her breakfast—she only had a cup of coffee, anyway—at a little table by the phone in the hall. That's when most of the calls came in and she had to be around to take them.

The phone rang and I heard her say: "I'm sorry, Inspector, he's not available just at the moment."

She meant Daddy, I expect. I could hear his bath running.

"Yes, *he's* here," Mandy was saying. "Just a minute." And she called: "Dr. Kendall! Detective Inspector Robens for you."

Dr. Kendall got up and went out to the hall. I hid behind my comic, but I was listening.

I heard him say "Yes, she's a patient," then "Good God!" I could faintly hear the other voice crackling on. Dr. Kendall said "Yes" a couple of times, then put down the phone.

"What's the matter?" Mandy said.

He kept his voice low, but I've got sharp ears. "Lesley Peterson's been found strangled."

"Is Lesley *dead*?" I shouted. And I began to laugh. I couldn't help it.

CHAPTER 3

The rector announced it at assembly. You should have heard the buzz that went round, even though most of us knew already. Some girls were crying—Pat Richards and that lot. I didn't see Anne Ridley, somebody said the police were questioning her.

I didn't feel anything. Well, I mean, Lesley had never been nice to me, and there's no use pretending, is there?

We were sent home straight from assembly, a whole holiday, so that was something at least. I took Bess to the golf course, I sneaked out while Mummy was on the phone. She'd never have let me go.

The cops turned us back. There were hundreds and *hundreds* of them poking among the bushes.

They'd found Lesley in the whins about the same spot as Jan. When she didn't come home after the pictures, her dad phoned the police and the first place they looked was the golf course.

She was starkers, just like Jan, and they found her clothes in a bunker. She hadn't been raped, just strangled—same as Jan again.

Whoever did it must have taken her in a car. I mean, it's *miles* from the Regent and nowhere near where Lesley lived. She'd never have walked all that way.

Daddy thinks he saw the car coming away after the murder. He was driving up to the clubhouse after seeing a patient. It was half-past ten and he noticed this car crawling up the dirt road that leads down to the big shed where Lesley was found. It had no lights on and Daddy just thought it was a courting couple. He's told the police now.

But I kept my mouth shut about the car *I* saw in Piper Lane. Well, I couldn't describe it anyway, and I never saw the driver, not properly, so what good could it do? Mummy was nearly round the twist as it was, she'd have done her nut if she'd known I was on the streets at that time of night.

So I said I'd come straight home from Guides. Mummy would never have found out because Mandy doesn't blab, I'll give her that. But that fool, Helen Potts, had to open her big mouth. I could have *slaughtered* her! So it all came out about the pictures, but I still never mentioned the car. There was something scary about that car, or maybe it was the driver—I don't know why, because I definitely hadn't *seen* anything. I mean it was dark. . . .

People were in a flap in Chalford. My mother wouldn't even let me go to school alone, I had to call for Chrissie Forsyth across the road and promise to come home with her. Of course, I never did—I can't *stand* Chrissie.

I never got out after dark at all. No more pictures, no more Guides even. It was lousy.

I mean, it was so *pointless*. I'm not like Jan Allen or Lesley Peterson, no strange man would talk *me* into going with him. And if he tried any funny business, I'd sort him, I'm very strong.

It's funny to switch on T.V. and see pictures of your own town. They made even more of a thing this time than when Jan Allen was done in. You couldn't *move* for T.V. cameras and reporters.

They even came to our school at break to talk to Lesley's friends. But Miss Carey came out and chased them.

It said in the papers the police were conducting a house-to-house enquiry. I asked Uncle Ben what that meant, and he said policemen would go round the houses and question every person in town. About where they'd been on Monday night and so on.

"Even children? Even me?"

"Even you, pet. So have a good story ready."

It wasn't funny. I was scared I'd give myself away about that car I saw.

But they didn't come to Tramore Avenue for a day or two and I stopped worrying.

Daddy was visiting Lesley's parents every day to give them dope or something. On Wednesday at lunch he said to Mandy: "That boy you used to know—the brother—Keith, is it?"

"Kenneth."

"Yes, well he'd like to see you."

Kenny used to be keen on Mandy ages ago, but he chucked her. He's at university now and he's got hair down to his shoulders and a beard. He looks *grotty*.

Mandy went round that evening. When she came home, I said: "Well, is he going to take you back?"

"Kenny? God forbid! No, he's been hunting for Lesley's diary. Do you know where she kept it? Has she a locker at school? . . ."

What a shock! I'd clean forgotten that diary. It was still in my school-bag.

"Diary? What diary?"

Mandy stared at me. "But you *must* know she wrote a diary. Remember how she used to talk about it in Sunday school?"

"Well, I never heard her."

It was *stupid* to tell lies to Mandy, she was too smart. I should have said Lesley kept it in her school-bag and that would have satisfied her. Now I'd got her suspicious.

She said: "Kenny's found all the old ones, up to the end of June. But the current one's missing."

"So what? It's a load of crap anyway."

"So you do know about it? You've read it?"

"No, I *haven't*. I just know the stupid rot Lesley would write."

Mandy was still staring. "Celia, this could be important. If you know where that diary is—"

"Well, I don't, so get off my back, will you?"

I went out and slammed the door.

Back in my room I took the diary out of my bag and turned to September 14, the page with all the tiny writing crammed in.

I began to read. "Big adventure tonight. Anne's for tea, stayed too late, nearly dark when I came out. Got picked up! . . ."

Mandy's voice said: "Interesting, is it?"

She'd opened the door so quietly I hadn't heard her.

"Get out!" I screamed. "This is my room, you've no right—"

"Give me the diary, Celia."

"No!"

She started towards me. I said: "Stay where you are or I'll rip it up." I meant it, too.

Mandy sat down on the end of the bed. "Let's talk about it," she said.

"There's nothing to talk about."

"Aren't you interested in who killed Janice and Lesley?"

"Not much."

"Or Dr. Kendall?"

"Nobody killed him—he killed himself."

"Did he? That's not what the police think now."

She's clever, Mandy, she'd got me interested.

"What's the diary got to do with it?" I said.

So she explained. Or tried to—I didn't follow it all. Something about a letter Terry wrote just before he died. Mandy and the new Dr. Kendall worked out from the letter that he must have seen something happen, or nearly happen, to Lesley Peterson.

"What do you mean—'nearly happen'?" I asked.

"Mark Kendall thinks it was an attempt on her life. But the diary might tell us. September 14 was the date . . . Oh there *is* something, is there?" My face must have given me away.

"Well, if there is, *you're* not seeing it."

"Celia, this isn't a game. Two girls have been murdered, Terry Kendall, too, probably. Don't fool around—"

When she made her move, it was like lightning. She'd grabbed the diary out of my hand before I knew what she was up to.

I was *wild!* I pummelled away at her and got it back quite easily. But she held onto me.

We were half out of the door when Dr. Kendall appeared and pulled us apart. "What's going on?" he said.

"Just get that book from Celia, please." Mandy's glasses had fallen off and there was a scratch on her cheek.

They were two to one. I hadn't a hope now. So I threw the diary on the floor.

Dr. Kendall picked it up and then saw Mandy's glasses. "Pity these aren't broken, Mandy."

He had a point. She could look smashing if she wanted to, but she doesn't. I guess that's what Uncle Ben meant when he said Mandy and I have a lot in common. We go our own way and don't give a damn what other people think. Only I'm not soppy like Mandy, you'd never catch me helping in a children's hospital.

She just said, "Thank you, Dr. Kendall," in that tight voice, as if she loathed his guts.

"I've told you before, Mandy, the name is Mark."

She didn't bother answering that one. She said: "This is Lesley Peterson's diary. Celia found it."

"How—"

"Never mind how. Let's read it." We followed her into my room and she opened the exercise book and began to flick over the pages.

Dr. Kendall looked at me. "I hardly think that Celia—"

Mandy stopped him. "Celia found it, she's had plenty of opportunity to see what's in it."

Dr. Kendall didn't say any more so we looked at the diary together. After the bit I'd already read it went on: ". . . The old line—'Can I give you a lift home, my dear? Have a chocolate. You don't mind if we go round by the golf club—I've a call to make.' And I fell for it! But, of course, it wasn't a *stranger*. And how could I ever guess. . . . Well, we took the wrong turning, and there we were in the dark, quite near where Jan was found! I thought I'd had it. When I saw Dr. K. and the dog crossing the golf course, I shouted myself hoarse. What a *fool* I must have sounded—for it was all perfectly innocent. We drove straight home. Excitement here too: Dad had taken ill at the club and Mother was trying to phone the doctor. Never told them anything. . . . And so to bed."

"It fits," Dr. Kendall said. "Exactly what we thought."

"Pity she doesn't mention the man's *name,* though," Mandy said.

"Maybe further on. . . ."

We read the rest of the diary, right up to last Monday, the day she died.

But the only other bit was on September 22: "Called at Dr. K.'s surgery for prescriptions for Dad. Nearly spoke of what happened last week, but took cold feet."

"It's somebody Lesley *knew*," Mandy said. "She says it wasn't a stranger. The police'll have to see the diary."

"Yes," Dr. Kendall agreed. "Even Robens could hardly ignore *this*."

I was getting that scary feeling again. I was thinking of the car in Piper Lane, I was seeing the door open, and the driver. . . . I shut out the picture.

When I came home from school on Thursday, Mummy was talking to a policeman, a big man with three stripes on his sleeve.

"You're late, Celia," she said.

"I had to wait for Chrissie." That was a lie—I hadn't seen Chrissie Forsyth all day.

"Well, this . . . gentleman wants to ask you some questions." She made it sound like he was dirt. That was the way she always spoke to shopkeepers and tradesmen and people like that.

"Thanks for your help, Mrs. Armitage," the sergeant said.

"Don't badger Celia, remember. She's not strong." And she left us.

I wished she'd lay off that line about me not being strong. Uncle Ben said it was a defence mechanism because I was behind at school—I haven't a clue what he was on about.

Well, this sergeant had a long list of questions, everybody in Chalford was having to answer them. It was dead easy, because he was a dumb oaf, I could have told him the moon was blue and he'd just have written it down and gone on to the next question.

I stuck to the truth about Monday night, except I never mentioned Piper Lane or the car. It wasn't a lie at all, really, I just left it out.

But the copper wasn't so dumb. "So you were walking up High Street about ten o'clock, Celia?"

"That's right."

"Then you must have crossed Piper Lane?"

"Yes." Gosh, that gave me a fright! Why were they asking about Piper Lane? Then I remembered Anne Ridley had probably seen the car and told them.

"Did you notice anything unusual in the lane?"

"What sort of thing?"

"Well . . . anything at all."

"No."

"Like a car, maybe?"

"I wasn't really *looking*, Sergeant." I even remembered to call him sergeant.

And he wrote it all down, the big dumb oaf, and I stuck my tongue out while his head was bent.

It was dead easy.

The inquest was on Friday morning. I wasn't allowed to go—it was school as usual, worse luck! But not for Anne Ridley, she was at the inquest, giving evidence.

When she came back in the afternoon, the other girls were all round her, asking questions, drinking in everything she said. And, brother, was she making the most of it!

Just because she was the last person to see Lesley alive. And she wasn't *really* the last—*I'd* seen Lesley running up the lane, I'd even seen the murderer get out of his car and pull her in. Gosh, if I told them that, they'd have to listen to me!

When we came out at four, they were at it again, Anne and Pat Richards and two or three others. I heard Anne say: ". . . about half way up the lane, with no lights on. The police think somebody was maybe waiting for Lesley in that car, but I don't believe it—"

"Well, it's true," I said. I couldn't stop myself.

They all stared at me. "What do *you* know about it?" Pat said, in the same tone Mummy had used to the policeman. She was the little mousy one, always sucking up to the others. Janice had been her favourite, now it was Anne. A proper *stink*.

"I saw it happen," I said. "He opened the car door and Lesley bumped into it, then he got out and helped her in."

Some of them laughed.

Anne didn't laugh. "Where exactly was the car parked, Celia?"

"Just opposite the entrance to McKenzie's warehouse. It was facing up the way and I think it was partly on the pavement."

Anne said: "You're absolutely right."

You should have seen their faces! It felt great to be part of the action.

One girl said: "You actually *saw* the murderer?"

"Yes."

"What did he look like?"

"Well, of course, I was at the High Street corner, it was too far to see him *clearly*." But as I spoke, it was all coming back. I saw that car door opening. . . .

"He was tall," I said, "quite young, dark hair, small moustache, and he had a dark overcoat on." Yes, the picture was getting clearer. Why on earth had I been so scared to remember it before?

Somebody said: "Sounds like Peeping Tom." And they giggled.

Again Anne didn't join in. "Why on earth didn't you tell the police all this, Celia? They didn't know at the inquest."

"Oh, but I *did*. I told that big sergeant yesterday." Actually I *would* have if I'd remembered it as clearly then.

We stood at the school gate talking for *ages*. I really felt like I was one of them, it was *super*.

Mummy nearly had kittens by the time I got home. But she cheered up when I told her I'd been with Anne and Pat and that lot.

Lesley was buried on Saturday afternoon. St. Margaret's was packed to the door for the service, I've never *seen* so many people in the church.

The whole of Lesley's class were there—they'd kept a couple of pews down near the front. Although I wasn't in her form, Anne Ridley asked me to sit beside her. She's really quite nice, not stuck up at all. Pat Richards was *furious*, she had to sit in the row behind.

Nearly all the teachers were there, too. Anne nudged me. "There's your dark overcoat," she whispered, nodding at Peeping Tom. "I bet the police are watching him." He was two rows in front, beside Miss Carey, and with that moustache and the dark hair and the black coat—well, it *could* have been him.

He's a horrible, horrible, *horrible* man. He always picks on me in class, just because I'm slow. "Well, now, Miss Armitage, what pearls of wisdom have you for us today?" And he peers at the girls' legs when they go up the stairs. Oh, I could *kill* him! I can't think why Uncle Ben likes him, but they're always together—fishing or playing chess or something.

The Reverend Tyfield droned on and on, he's such a *bore*. Anne cried most of the time, but not me. I was gazing at the coffin with Lesley inside it and wondering where she was and whether she knew all these people were here, just for her. She'd have loved that, she was so stuck up.

Well, there she was in her coffin. That's where all her cleverness landed her, in a coffin. And I was alive!

When we got out, there was a big crowd on the street, with lots of cameramen and T.V. crews. And there were *dozens* of cars behind the hearse. Must have been the biggest funeral in Chalford for years.

As I watched, a voice said in my ear: "Celia, I want to ask you a few questions." It was Detective Inspector Robens, the one who'd questioned me at the time Jan Allen was killed. He was a friend of Mandy's.

He was gazing at the line of cars and the people getting in, not looking at me at all. The coffin was in the hearse now and they were squeezing the wreaths in all round it. But there were too many, and some had to be put in another car. *That* would have pleased Lesley, if she'd known.

Kenny and his other sister were helping their parents into the car behind the hearse. The mother and father looked doped—I suppose Daddy had given them something. Daddy himself was weird in top hat and mourning suit.

At last they moved off. Inspector Robens took out his cigarettes, he smokes like a furnace.

"Well, young Celia," he said, "how about an ice-drink or something?"

Gosh, this was the red carpet! I mean, he could easily just have spoken to me there on the street.

We went to Rixi's in Church Square. We were the only customers, it was too early in the afternoon.

I got a double sundae—they're *super* at Rixi's—and the inspector had tea or coffee or something.

He smoked all the time, just one fag after another.

"How's Mandy?" he said.

"She's O.K."

"A real nice girl." He's soft about Mandy because she'd helped when his daughter was ill. She died in the end—polio, I think it was. He goes to our church and Mandy's a great one for visiting the sick.

He said: "Celia, you told Sergeant Ellison you saw nothing in Piper Lane last Monday."

"Yes."

"Well, I hear you've been spreading a different story at school."

I bet that was Pat Richards. Stinking little sneak! I was quite glad, all the same, because I *wanted* to tell, now I knew it was Peeping Tom I'd seen.

I said: "When I was talking to the policeman, I didn't remember. It came back later."

He stubbed out a fag, lit another, and began to cough. Then he said: "It sure did. Tall, dark, young, with a moustache, and wearing a black overcoat—right?"

"Yes."

"The girl you saw running up the lane, it was Lesley, was it?"

"It *must* have been."

"But you did recognise her?"

"No, it was too far away, but—"

"That car—it was parked opposite McKenzie's gate, you said?"

"Just about."

"That's eighty-three yards exactly from High Street. The nearest lamp's thirty yards up the lane. No wonder you didn't recognise the girl." He coughed again.

"Well, so what?"

"You couldn't have seen much of the man either, not at that distance and in that light."

"All right, don't believe me." That was all the thanks you got for trying to help. I could see that man's face as clear as day. And it was Peeping Tom Baines.

"Celia, what *did* you see?"

I just got up and walked out—I hadn't even finished my sundae. I was *mad!* I mean, you'd think they'd have been glad to get such a good description.

I ran all the way home but he didn't come after me.

CHAPTER 4

Miss Carey has started coming to dinner again, last night was the second time in a week. I guess she's got a thing going with Dr. Kendall, just like she had with his brother, Terry. Mandy hates her like stink—I know why, because Terry was keen on Mandy until Miss Carey came along.

I think she's O.K.—I mean, for a *teacher.* All teachers are lousy, but Miss Carey's not so rotten as most. She doesn't *pick* on me, the way Peeping Tom does. Some of the girls are goofy about her, Lesley was *the* goofiest.

Mummy likes Miss Carey, it was Mummy who kept inviting her here when Terry Kendall stayed with us. Just to spite Mandy.

I don't know if I told you, but Mummy and Mandy get in each other's hair. Of course, she's not Mandy's mother, really, just her stepmother, and I expect that's the reason. Uncle Ben says Mummy's jealous, but that's daft. Why would anyone be jealous of Mandy? She's got *nothing.*

Well, anyway, Miss Carey was here for dinner last night. There was a lot of talk about the murders, nobody in Chalford can think of anything else. Mummy's *furious* because they haven't caught the man yet, she thinks the police are a dead loss. So does Dr. Kendall. He said he'd warned them Lesley was in danger and they'd done nothing about it.

Mandy didn't like that. "How do you know they did nothing?" she said. "You're just guessing."

"I know I warned Robens on Saturday and she was dead on the Monday."

Daddy said: "Well, they've called in the regional squad now—

Egmont's taken over. Hugh Robens hasn't been the same since he lost that child of his. They say he's drinking."

Mandy nearly hit the roof. "That's not true either! He smokes a lot but he doesn't drink."

"There's no need to be *rude*, darling." This was Mummy, she never misses a chance to get a dig in.

And Miss Carey said: "What a pretty dress, Mandy, I don't think I've seen that one before." If she imagined *that* was smoothing things over, she was up a gum tree. Mandy was wearing her sweetie pink thing and she'd had it for *years*.

Oh, it was super listening to them all having a go at Mandy! They'd forgotten I was there.

But they were soon back to the murders. Dr. Kendall was explaining where the police had gone wrong. When his brother fell over the cliff, they'd been too quick to button up the case—Terry Kendall had murdered Jan Allen and then killed himself.

"I *knew* that couldn't be right," he said. "That's why I stayed on in Chalford, to see justice done."

No wonder he rubs Mandy the wrong way—he sounded like he was God speaking. Uncle Ben says some doctors get like that, they look down their noses at the rest of the world.

"Actually," Dr. Kendall said, "somebody else knew it, too." He took his wallet from his pocket and showed us a piece of paper. "It's a photocopy," he said, "of a note delivered to my hotel the night I arrived. The original's with the police and they've done damn all about it."

He read it out—I could see it was in big capital letters: "'YOUR BROTHER DIDN'T FALL, HE WAS PUSHED.' Who do you think could have written that?"

Nobody answered. Mandy was pouring coffee, and there wasn't a sound except for the chink of cups.

I don't usually wait for coffee, I *hate* the stuff, but I sat on tonight, hoping nobody would notice me.

Finally Mandy said: "If it wasn't a practical joke—"

"It wasn't that, I'm sure."

"Well, then, it sounds as if someone actually *saw* him being pushed."

"That's what I think. But who could that be? Who else would be around at that time in the morning? Apart from the murderer, I mean?"

There was another ghastly silence and then Mandy came in again: "The person Terry was going to meet."

But now Mummy remembered me at last. "Celia! You should have been upstairs long ago!"

I wasn't budging now. "Don't be wet, Mummy, I'm not an *infant!* I know what Terry was up to when he took the dog out at night. He was meeting his prostitute." I loved that word, even though I wasn't sure *exactly* what it meant.

"Celia!" It was Daddy this time, but I just sat tight. I knew they'd never actually *do* anything about shifting me.

So after a while the conversation started again. Miss Carey said: "If you're suggesting Terry was meeting Meg that night, that's rubbish. He'd given her up *weeks* before."

"You're wrong, Shelagh." I think Mandy enjoyed correcting her. "You actually heard him make the date. We were having dinner in this very room when she rang, remember?"

"No, I don't remember."

Gosh, but I did! I took the call upstairs and I came down and told Terry there was a lady for him on the phone. I never guessed it was his *prostitute!*

Mandy was in the kitchen, I remember, getting the coffee or something. The rest of them were sitting round the table—Mummy and Daddy, Terry, the Cohens, Uncle Ben and Miss Carey. Oh, and Peeping Tom—I nearly forgot him.

Dr. Kendall said in a very funny voice: "You mean Meg rang here during that dinner party? And you all heard Terry arrange to meet her later on?"

"*I* never heard it," Miss Carey said.

"Well, I did." Mandy sounded like she didn't believe her. "He left this door open and you couldn't help overhearing. 'Usual place,' he said, 'but it'll have to be late—half-past twelve.' Knowing Terry, it was easy to guess what he was up to. . . . What's the matter, Dr. Kendall?" He was staring at her like he'd had a shock. He said: "Well, you see, one thing that's puzzled me is

how the murderer knew he'd find Terry on the golf course that
night. Especially so *late*."

I couldn't think why they all looked so *shattered*. As if he was
accusing them or something.

Daddy said: "Be careful what you're saying, Kendall." He was
breathing like his asthma was troubling him.

Even Miss Carey was upset. "Yes, I must say, Mark, that's
uncalled for. All of us who were here that night were Terry's
friends."

"Yes, I know. It was one of his friends who killed him."

Gosh, this was *super!* It was more exciting than "Star Trek."

Mummy said: "Just because of a phone call some of us may or
may not have overheard, you dare to suggest—"

"No, not only that, Mrs. Armitage. There's other evidence."

Daddy slipped a pill into his mouth. "Let's hear it."

Dr. Kendall produced another paper from his wallet. "Shelagh
and Mandy know about this," he said. "The others probably don't.
It's a letter to me that Terry started but didn't finish—I found it
after his death. Shall I read it?"

Nobody stopped him, so he did. " 'One night—a week ago last
Tuesday—I saw something, innocent in itself, but if you relate it
to what happened earlier—No, I can't bring myself to put it
down on paper, it's too horrible, it *must* be false. . . . Yet I can't
leave it there, for it does tie up with what I thought I saw last
July. Suppose it were true—what a load to have on my conscience! Twice I nearly questioned the girl—when I saw her next
day, and again when she came to the surgery last night. But—'
And that's where it stops. Mandy will tell you what he was referring to—she and I worked it out."

Mandy said: "There was an attempt on Lesley Peterson's life in
September. Or at least it looked as if it was going to be. Terry
appeared on the scene just in time to stop it." She explained what
we'd found in Lesley's diary.

"Nothing actually happened?" Mummy said. "He just saw
Lesley and some man sitting in a car?"

"Yes."

"Well, why should there be anything wrong in that?"

"Because it was dark, and the car was parked not ten yards from where Janice Allen's body was found."

"Yet neither of them reported it—neither Lesley nor Terry?"

"It was someone Lesley knew and trusted—she said so in her diary. She couldn't *believe* there had been any evil intention."

"And Terry?"

Dr. Kendall took over from Mandy. "I believe it was someone *he* knew and trusted, too."

Miss Carey said: "You're reading too much into this, Mark. We all know what Terry was like—a ditherer; he hated making decisions. So long as there was any doubt, he'd do nothing."

"But remember what he said, Shelagh: 'It's too horrible, it *must* be false.' What's too horrible? The suspicion there had nearly been a second murder? Why did that *have* to be false? There was a sadistic killer on the loose, it was on the cards he'd strike again. Terry must have known that."

"So?"

"So he recognised the killer, it was a friend. And *that's* what he found too horrible to believe, *that's* why he couldn't bring himself to denounce him."

Gwen said: "And what's this bit about last July?"

"I'd guess that's a reference to the first murder. He must have seen something that night."

Mandy nodded. "I think he did. He passed Abbot's Creek just after the other girls left Janice Allen. He didn't see Janice. When I asked him if he'd noticed any cars he started to tell me something, then changed his mind . . ."

They'd all finished their coffee ages ago, but nobody made any move to leave the table. The room was thick with smoke and I nearly burst trying not to cough. They'd forgotten about me again.

Daddy said: "So you've decided it's one of us? Or rather, one of the people at the dinner party here the night your brother was killed?"

"That's right, Dr. Armitage." Oh, he was *cool,* and he didn't even *see* they were all furious. Well, except maybe Mandy. I was loving every minute.

Of course, I knew who the murderer was, no need for *me*

to get steamed up. It was Mr. Baines, Peeping Tom. I mean, *he* was at that dinner party, that proved it, didn't it? And I'd seen him in Piper Lane that night, whatever that stinking Inspector Robens might say.

They weren't finished yet. *He* wasn't, anyway—Dr. Kendall, I mean. He was talking about Meg now, Terry's prostitute. "It's absurd," he said, "that the police haven't traced her yet."

"What makes you think they haven't?" Mandy asked.

"They haven't told me."

"Why ever should they?"

"Well, it was I who suggested to them that Meg had written the anonymous note."

Mandy laughed. "Do you really believe they couldn't have worked *that* out for themselves? You haven't a monopoly of wisdom, Dr. Kendall."

"There's no need to be *rude*, Mandy." Mummy's parrot cry.

Mandy went on just the same: "I bet Hugh Robens not only knows who Meg is, he'll have found all *she* knows on the subject of Terry's death. . . . Shocking, of course, that he hasn't reported to *you*."

She'd really scored that time, he turned quite red.

Miss Carey said: "Mark, did you mean that about going for a walk after dinner? My head's splitting."

"Yes, indeed. I'd love to."

"Keep away from the golf course," Mandy said. "It's getting a reputation."

I nipped over to Uncle Ben's without telling anyone I was going. Mummy would be round the twist when she missed me—well, who cared? It was only nine o'clock, lots of girls my age get staying out far later than that.

I *had* to see Uncle Ben. I hadn't twigged half what I'd heard tonight, but he'd sort it out, he was super at that.

He has a flat on Northcliffe Road, above Lauderdale the jeweller. When he came to Chalford at first, he used to live in our house, just like Dr. Kendall does now. I was still a baby and I don't remember it. Then there was some big row and he moved out—I've never heard what it was about, he won't tell me, neither will Mummy or Daddy.

What I like about Uncle Ben's flat is the way you feel *comfortable* in it. I mean, if somebody drops ash on the carpet, well, so what? Uncle Ben doesn't mind. It makes a change from the way Mummy keeps our house, like it was a museum.

Tonight there was a newspaper on the floor and the supper dishes hadn't been cleared from the table. Uncle Ben was smoking his pipe and watching T.V.

He gave me a big hug and a kiss—I never let anyone else kiss me, not even Mummy.

"Have a chocolate, pet," he said. He always has chocolates for me, he eats a lot himself. "Does your mother know you're here?"

"Yes."

He laughed. "You're the world's worst liar." He went over and phoned Mummy. I knew it would be all right now I was *here*, she never minded me being with Uncle Ben.

"Yes, surely," I heard him say. "I'll bring her home, Gwen. See you later." He rang off.

"She was nearly calling the police," he told me.

"She *would*."

"You can't blame her—not after what's happened. . . . Here, let's have a look at you." He peered into my face. "I thought so. Never mind, we'll sort it out."

He went into the bedroom.

"I'm all right," I called. But I wasn't. I can tell when an attack's coming on—I feel *high*, just like that time I drank a whole glass of sherry. I always feel mad at Daddy when I get my asthma—I mean, it was his fault really, that's who I got it from.

Uncle Ben came back with his syringe and gave me a shot in the arm. "All right, let's be having it. What brought it on this time? Cats, plants, or just plain excitement?"

"Excitement, I guess." I told him all about the talk tonight at dinner. I'm very good at *remembering* things, even when I don't twig them. I once learned the names of all the books in the Bible, from Genesis straight through. I think I could still say them. I don't see how I'm *really* stupid when I can do that. And Uncle Ben agrees.

He listened to my story right through. That's one of the things I like about Uncle Ben, he's always interested, he's not just pretending, like Mummy.

He asked a lot of questions, about what everybody said, and so on. It all became clearer in my head as we went on, it's funny how just *talking* to Uncle Ben can do that for me.

Finally he said: "Well, I guess Dr. Kendall won't be popular after *that* diagnosis!"

"Oh, they were *furious,* Uncle Ben—even Miss Carey. And she's nuts about him, absolutely *nuts.*"

He laughed. "Well, he's worth trying to hook. Mark Kendall's going places, no question about it."

"He's not half as good a doctor as you are."

"Nice of you to say so, pet, but it's not true. . . . Have a chocolate." He pushed the box across. "And tell me what else is on your mind."

I chose one with a hard centre. "Nothing else," I said, keeping my eyes down. It's not *fair,* the way he can read my thoughts.

"As I said, you're a rotten liar."

So, of course, I had to tell him, though I knew he'd be upset. Old Baines is a friend of his, I just can't *think* why. The only time I've ever made Uncle Ben angry was when I told him Baines's nickname. Well, I mean, *everyone* calls him Peeping Tom at school, I thought it would make Uncle Ben laugh. But he was *furious.*

So I knew he wouldn't like to hear his friend was a murderer.

But he didn't argue or anything, this time he *did* laugh. "You'll have to do better than that, pet," he said.

"It's true! I'm not telling lies, I *did* see him in that car!"

"Oh, I dare say you *think* you did. But your subconscious can play tricks, Celia, it can substitute a false picture in your memory for something it doesn't want you to remember."

"I don't understand a word you're saying." I was sulking.

"Well, never mind. . . . Anyway, if Tom Baines did one murder, he presumably did the others as well?"

"Yes."

"And the attempt on Lesley last month—the one you told me about that she mentioned in her diary—that must have been, Tom, too?"

"Yes." I didn't spot the trap.

"You think she would accept a lift in his car at night?"

Gosh, no, I hadn't thought of that! Lesley had absolutely loathed Peeping Tom, she couldn't bear to be near him.

I was back in the corner of High Street looking down Piper Lane and seeing the car door open. The driver's face was in shadow again and I got that queer, shivery feeling I had before. . . .

Uncle Ben was watching me, he knows my mind better than I do myself. He said: "I've got ginger beer or lemonade or—"

"I'll have ginger beer, please."

I was getting sleepy—that was the injection.

"Uncle Ben," I said, "tell me my sucking story."

He often used to tell me stories at bed-time. My favourite was always about Tramore Avenue when he went there at first. I was allowed to suck my thumb while I listened.

"Once upon a time," he said, "there was a young doctor called Ben Radford who got his first job in Chalford. And he lived in the house of the senior partner, Dr. Armitage, and it was the loveliest house he'd ever seen. Now the Armitages had two daughters—"

"You've missed out a bit, Uncle Ben. About Mummy." He often had to be reminded of this part.

"Oh yes! Well, Mrs. Armitage was very beautiful and charming and kind and she and her husband entertained nearly every evening and they were the most popular couple in the whole of Chalford."

"Was it really like that?"

"Yes, it was really like that." Gosh! How things had changed!

He went on with the story. "Now the Armitages had two daughters. The elder one, Mandy (she was Mrs. Armitage's *stepdaughter*) was nine and the younger one, Celia, was just a tiny little baby in a cot."

"Tell me about Mandy," I said. I was already sucking my thumb, I couldn't help it.

"Mandy? She was a solemn, solitary little girl with pigtails, always playing with her dolls."

"And Celia?" This was the bit I loved.

"Celia was the sweetest little bundle of nonsense Ben Radford had ever seen."

"Was I really like that, Uncle Ben?"

"Yes, you were a lovely baby. Lovely and cuddly. With dimples and everything and you were always chuckling and smiling."

"What went wrong, then?"

"That's not in the script."

"Mummy and Daddy were lousy parents, weren't they? Or was there something rotten in me from the start?"

But, of course, he wouldn't answer that. "Time you were home in bed, pet. I'll just get my coat."

The doorbell rang. Uncle Ben looked a bit put out as he went to answer it.

There were voices in the hall, then who should come in but Peeping Tom!

"Ah! the fair Miss Armitage!" he said. "I trust you've done your history prep. for tomorrow?"

"Oh yes, sir." What a hope!

Uncle Ben said: "Mr. Baines just called to return a book." I didn't see the book, he must have left it in the hall. "Well, Celia, if you'll put your coat on . . ."

I picked up my anorak from the floor. "I can go home by myself."

"Nonsense." He was practically pushing me out the door. "Set up the board, Tom. We'll have time for one game when I get back." Gosh! Imagine starting to play chess after ten o'clock at night!

In the car I said: "I'm sorry, Uncle Ben, but I just can't like Mr. Baines."

He nodded. "His conversational style requires an adult taste. Tom's all right, though."

"And I *still* think he's a murderer."

He swung the car into our drive. "You don't really, pet, do you?"

He was right, I didn't. I wished I did.

CHAPTER 5

Well, the days passed and nothing happened and it got *boring*. Chalford dropped out of the T.V. news, and there wasn't so much in the papers either.

Anyway people had got tired of seeing pictures of these whins on the golf course. Just for a change the *Express* one day had a photo of Jan Allen and Lesley Peterson *together*—it was one taken when they got their medals as joint dux of the junior school two years ago. And the bit underneath said they were almost like twins, there was only two days between them. That was news to me, I knew Lesley was a day younger than me, I didn't know Jan's birthday was so close. What a coincidence!

The town was still crawling with policemen, I don't know what they were all doing. Everybody was talking about it—I mean it was *wild* that a man could get away with three murders like that, what were we paying our police *for?* You only had to say the word "police" and Mummy nearly had a fit. Of course, she was scared I'd be the next body in the bushes.

There was a *super* row one day between Dr. Kendall and Mandy. It happened at breakfast, there was nobody there except Dr. Kendall and me. Usually he reads his *Times* and never says a word, but this morning he said: "Celia, you remember the night Lesley Peterson died?"

"Uh-huh?"

"What time did you get home?"

"I don't remember. Quarter-past ten or so, I guess. Why?"

"Who all were here when you got back?"

"Just Mandy."

"Your mother and father were both out?"

But just then Mandy came dashing in with a face like thunder. Dr. Kendall must have forgotten she was in her usual place by the phone in the hall.

"How dare you!" she said—she was hopping mad. "That's absolutely *despicable*. Asking a child to spy on her own parents!"

"I was only checking, Mandy."

"Well, check some other way—or leave it to those whose job it is."

"A damn poor job they're making of it."

"Oh yes, you know better than the experts."

He was just about as angry. "The bloody experts convicted my brother of murder and suicide. Without a trial. And then had to eat their words. . . . I'm determined to get at the truth. I was fond of Terry."

Mandy looked him straight in the eye. "It wasn't obvious," she said.

"What?"

"Those letters you used to write him from the States, he showed me some of them. There wasn't much affection in *them*."

I turned over a page of my comic so they would think I wasn't tuned in.

They'd both calmed down a bit. Dr. Kendall said: "Shelagh didn't like them either. Priggish, you'd say they were? Condescending?"

" 'Smug' would be my word."

"You don't understand, Mandy. In some ways Terry never grew up. He had a schoolboy's attitude to right and wrong. Unless you had expressly forbidden something, Terry considered he had a licence to do it. You had to spell everything out. That's why I was always lecturing him."

"It didn't sound right from a younger brother."

"*Someone* had to do it. Father gave up latterly, and anyway he died soon afterwards. Terry was very weak, he needed to be kept on the rails. He knew it himself, he never held it against me. Although we were so different, we got on well, Terry and I."

"So he used to tell me. Reading those letters of yours, I could never understand why."

"But you do now?"

She shrugged. "It doesn't excuse you questioning Celia about her parents."

"I promise not to do that again."

"Thank you, Dr. Kendall."

"Oh, for God's sake, Mandy, how many times do I have to tell you the name is *Mark*." And when she didn't answer: "My God, we live in the same house, we have our meals together, we work together—do we have to be so formal? Damnit, I'm not asking you to sleep in my *bed*."

I got such a shock I knocked over the packet of cornflakes. They both spun round—they'd forgotten me as usual.

I thought Mandy was going to hit the roof again. But suddenly she grinned and said: "O.K., Mark."

Of course, I knew why Mandy was playing it cool with Dr. Kendall. Uncle Ben has explained it to me. She's so scared people might think she's chasing a man that she puts KEEP OFF THE GRASS signs all round. I mean, that's what these glasses are, and the pony-tail. She's been had twice already and she's taking damn good care it doesn't happen a third time.

She could look terrific if she wanted, you should see her in a bikini, she's got a super figure. But the clothes she wears! It's not that she hasn't got taste, it's just—well, Uncle Ben calls it a psychological something or other.

Me, I don't know why she bothers. Men aren't worth it. I'm never going to marry, but I'll not spend my time thinking about it like Mandy must do.

Actually, I think she's quite interested in this Dr. Kendall, though she'd never, never, *never* admit it, specially now Miss Carey's got her hooks in. As for him, well, I don't know, he seems keen enough on Miss Carey, but maybe he just can't shake her off. In spite of being such a know-all, he should have a learner's permit as far as girls are concerned. He had one in America but she jilted him, he told us. My guess is that's been his only one.

It's really amazing, I used to think Anne Ridley was a stuck-up pig, just like Jan and Lesley and Pat Richards and the rest of that gang. But she's not at all. I've got to know her since that day of the inquest, and she's really *smashing*. Kids like Helen

Potts get to be a bore after a time—I mean, they're so *immature*, aren't they? I mean, after all, I'm exactly the same age as Pat and six weeks older than Anne.

Anne's got me accepted in the gang. Well, *most* of them accept me, but that stinking Pat Richards walks off with her nose in the air whenever I appear.

Of course, I've taken good care not to be "vicious" like the parents expect me to be. I've no need to be vicious now I'm in with the gang, I guess I was just jealous before.

We still talk about the murders. Well, I mean, it's natural, isn't it, when two of your friends have been snuffed out like that, one after the other.

Anne's terribly, terribly scared she'll be the next to go. And the police are giving her special protection, she says. The way she sees it, you have to be thirteen, you have to be in second form at Chalford Comprehensive, you have to be in the gang, and you have to be clever. That's not boasting—if you knew Anne, she's the *last* person to boast. But, now that Jan and Lesley are gone, she's way out on her own at the top of the class.

My one kick about Anne is, she's silly about boys. She's just copying that dumb sister of hers, Elma, the one that was supposed to see Lesley home from the pictures and went off on her boy friend's motor bike instead.

You'd think that would be a *lesson* to Anne. But no, she's got her eye on Willie Toshak in fourth form, the one with the fair, curly hair. Oh I suppose he's good-looking if you like that type, but he's *years* older than Anne—well, two at least.

When we walk home after school, she has to go round by Wellington Street just in the hope of passing Willie, and when we do, she pretends not to see him but her bottom wiggles even more than usual.

One day I said to her—I couldn't stop myself—"I think you're silly, chasing after that snotty boy."

"He's not a snotty boy!"

"Well, he's a *boy*, anyway."

"What's wrong with that?"

"Look what they grow up into."

Anne gave me a funny look. "You mean *men?*"

"Yes. I *hate* them." Well, all except Uncle Ben, he's different.

"You really have some potty ideas, Celia."

"Look what they did to Jan and Lesley. *There's* men for you."

"Or women."

"What?"

"Well, it *could* be a woman."

"Don't be silly, Anne. What woman would—"

"They weren't *raped*, you know. I read in a paper that the police say it could be a woman."

I don't know why but this made me *wild*. I just didn't want to listen.

But I daren't quarrel with Anne. I mean, I was really enjoying school for the first time, I even did some homework, Anne said I wasn't stupid at all, I just needed to work harder.

So we never talked about boys again, and when Willie Toshak stopped me one day and gave me a note for Anne, I passed it on even though I was *boiling* inside. You should have seen her face when I gave her it!

Soon it was the end of October and everyone was talking about Guy Fawkes Night. That's *the* night of the year in Chalford—well, maybe Christmas is even better, with the presents and all that. But they make a big thing of November 5. I mean, there's parties in people's gardens, with the guys being burnt and Catherine wheels and whatnot going off, then everybody joins a torchlight procession down to the Pier sands where there's a huge bonfire and more fireworks. It's organised by the Town Council or some such lot.

I'm not allowed to go since the terrible, *terrible* asthma I had after Guy Fawkes Night three years ago. I was carted off to hospital and nearly died! Uncle Ben said that excitement plus the smoke and the fumes had gone for me (smoke's one of the things I'm allergic to).

Anyway he said I mustn't ever go again. And that's one thing about Mummy, I can get my own way every time except where it's doctor's orders. Then she puts her foot down. Sometimes she almost sounds *pleased* when my asthma's bad, she loves talking about it so that people will know why I'm so far behind at school and difficult and all that.

Well, now that I was one of the gang, I was *determined* to go to the bonfire this year. All the others were going.

So I spoke to Uncle Ben.

He wasn't keen. "It's not worth it, pet," he said.

"But I was only a kid that last time, Uncle Ben. It wouldn't happen now. And if I did start to get high, I'd come home. Honestly!"

He grinned. "What a hope! . . . Oh, all right, we'll take a chance. I can give you a jag before you go."

"Oh super!" I gave him a big hug. "You'll tell Mummy?"

"Yes."

But Mummy said no. It wasn't my asthma that worried her this time, it was the strangler.

They nearly didn't have the bonfire this year, there was such a fuss in the *Citizen* about the danger, letters to the editor and all that jazz. In the end they decided to go ahead, but parents were told they should make sure there was some grown-up keeping an eye on their children.

"Who were you going with?" Mummy asked me. This was at lunch the day after I spoke to Uncle Ben. "Was it Helen Potts?"

"I wouldn't be seen dead with Helen Potts, she's an *infant*. I've been asked to Pat Richards' party and—"

"Pat Richards! Well, that's different, I must say. *They'll* not take any chances. Perhaps, if all the others are going . . ."

I didn't tell her I only got an invitation because Anne told Pat *she* wouldn't go unless I was invited, too.

Out of the blue Dr. Kendall said: "If I were you, Mrs. Armitage, I shouldn't let Celia go. It's too big a risk."

I glared at him. He should keep his big nose out of other people's business.

Daddy said: "Mandy'll go. She can keep an eye on Celia."

"I don't *want* Mandy," I said. "I can look after myself."

Mandy grinned at me. "Don't worry, Celia, I'll not cramp your style. I'll just be *there* in case I'm needed."

Well, let her come, if that made them happy. I'd soon shake her off.

I waited for Anne at the school gate at four to tell her it was all right for Friday. We met there every day and walked home together.

But today, I couldn't believe my eyes, she came out with Willie Toshak, giggling and laughing, and she just sailed past me. Well, she turned and waved and said, "Hi, Celia!" then she was giggling again, and her bottom was going from side to side, just like Elma's. I bet she practises in front of a mirror.

I was *mad!* I could have killed her! And while I was standing there like a knotless thread, Pat Richards said: "I shouldn't wait if I were you. They're going for a walk to the creek." And *she* giggled and ran away. A good job, too, or I'd have bashed her, I really would. I had to take an anti-histamine when I got home.

Well next day—Thursday—Anne came up at break, all smiles, and started to chat away as if nothing has happened. After a bit she said: "You're not sulking, Celia, are you?"

"Why should I?"

"I believe you *are*. Is it because of Willie?"

"I couldn't care less about Willie."

"He's fun, Celia, you'd like him. . . . Don't you think you and I have been seeing too much of each other? After all, we've both got lots of other friends."

Maybe *she* had. . . .

"See you at four today?" she said.

And she was there. We walked home together, we never saw Willie Toshak, his name was never mentioned. Everything was all right again.

Friday morning my eyes and nose were streaming with hay fever. I wasn't *wheezing*, but I took a pill just in case.

Uncle Ben came for lunch. I knew he was watching me, but I just kept my eyes down and never said a word.

Joke was, *Daddy's* asthma was going fit to kill. He was breathing like a concertina, and I saw him take a pill.

Uncle Ben said: "Going to be a fine night for the fireworks!"

That set Dr. Kendall off. "It's criminal that they're letting this go ahead. "It's an open invitation to the strangler."

Daddy didn't agree. "You'll never stop the kids having their fun on Guy Fawkes Night."

"If I were a parent in Chalford, I'd stop *my* kids from going out tonight, fun or no fun."

I was watching Mummy, scared she might change her mind even now. But though she looked worried, she didn't say anything. If it hadn't been for Pat Richards' party, I'm sure she'd have put her foot down.

The party was at half-past six. I called at Uncle Ben's on my way.

"Help yourself to a chocolate, pet," he said, as he got his syringe out. He looked a bit unhappy, too. "You'd really be far better at home watching the telly. Excitement's the worst thing for you."

"I'm O.K., Uncle Ben," I said as the needle went in.

"Well, look after yourself. You're the dangerous age, remember."

Yes, I'd worked that out, too. I mean, Anne Ridley was *sure* she would be the next to go, but what about me? I was the same age as Jan and Lesley, I was in the same school, and I was in the gang now too. I wasn't *clever*, like them, but maybe you didn't have to be clever.

I shivered when I thought of it, it wasn't really fear, more excitement. I mean, in a way I was almost hoping . . .

The party was *super*. The Richards have an enormous garden, with masses of trees and shrubs and a lawn as big as a field. We had a picnic outside, with hot dogs and chips and roasted chestnuts. We drank some kind of hot punch, Pat said it had real alcohol in it, but I guess she was just boasting as usual. I sat beside Anne all the time and it was super fun.

Afterwards Mr. Richards—he's a big, fat man always smoking a cigar—came out with a box of fireworks and let them off on the lawn. He's a bit bossy, he wouldn't let any of the young ones near them. But I was glad to keep back, I'm scared stiff of fireworks.

Mrs. Richards was around, too, but she just looked through me. She's one of the ones that thinks I'm vicious, she once complained to Daddy I'd thrown a stone at Pat. I hadn't really— Pat just got in the way, and anyway she wasn't hurt, she's just a cry-baby. Mummy was *livid* when she heard.

The bonfire on the beach was to be at nine o'clock. So at half-past eight Mr. Richards handed out torches—long sticks with some stuff at one end that burns for *ages*. The Richardses' guy was still smouldering away, so we stuck the end of our torches into the red embers, and they fizzled and crackled, then burst into flame and lit up the whole garden, as bright as day. There were sixteen of us and we all waved our torches about and shrieked and laughed. Oh, it was *super!*

We fooled around for a bit, then Mr. and Mrs. Richards decided we should leave. I was keeping close to Anne, because I knew Pat would barge in if she could, but luckily just when we were at the gate, somebody called Pat back so we dodged her.

As we made our way towards the pier, crowds were joining us all the time until we were one long procession of lights. There was no sound but the tramping of feet and the crackle and splutter of fireworks going off. Gosh, it was weird!

The smoke was making me cough and I felt just a *teeny* bit high, but nothing much, Uncle Ben's jag was marvellous. I wouldn't have missed this for *anything*.

I turned to say something to Anne, and she wasn't there! She'd been beside me just a minute before. . . .

Then I heard a giggle, I whipped my head round and there she was, disappearing back the way we'd come. Hand in hand with Willie Toshak!

Everything went black, I thought I was going to pass out. I felt so *mad!* I mean, what a dirty, sneaky way to do it! I loathed her, she was a stinking, stinking *pig*—worse than any of them, she was so two-faced.

We were on the beach, I was still walking, carrying my torch over my head, I hardly knew what I was doing. Soon the line broke up and we spread out round the big pile of logs and twigs and brushwood that had been here since yesterday morning. Someone was pouring petrol over it.

There were *hundreds* here already, and back as far as you could see, the waving line of torches was still coming on. I saw lots of coppers mingling with the crowd.

I felt lousy. But the more I thought about that sneaky pig, Anne Ridley, the madder I got. So I flung down my torch and started running back up towards the road.

I hadn't gone ten yards when a bobby stopped me. "Where are you off to, lass?"

"I'm feeling sick, I'm going home."

"You can't go home alone."

"My mother's just up the road," I gasped, and dodged round him and went on running.

Another copper stopped me before I reached High Street. After that they didn't bother me.

I was choking by then, and it was sore every breath I took. This was nearly as bad as that time three years ago. But when I'd rested for a bit, I felt better.

I tried to guess which way they'd gone. They would keep well away from the Pier sands, so as not to be seen. And they wouldn't want cops shining torches in their faces the way they'd done to me.

Abbot's Creek! That was it! That's where they were making for the other day, Pat Richards had said. The creek was a favourite spot of Anne's, I knew that. And we'd often seen her sister Elma and her boy friend snogging down there while we were swimming.

It was nearly a mile, but if it had been ten, I would still have gone. I was going to teach Anne Ridley a lesson she wouldn't forget in a hurry, I'd make her sorry for the rotten, sneaky way she'd treated me. I started to run again.

The sky was all lit up, they must have got their stupid bonfire going. I couldn't care less about that now.

I didn't even glance down Piper Lane when I crossed it. I just didn't want to remember that awful night last month. . . .

There was hardly anyone about. Twice I thought I heard footsteps following me, but when I looked round there was no one.

And once there was this *wild* breathing right in my ear. I nearly jumped out of my skin, till I realised it was my *own* breathing!

I had to stop running. I had a stitch and I was terribly out of breath. Uncle Ben would have a fit if he saw me, I was going to be a wreck tomorrow. But I didn't care. I was getting madder and madder all the time.

Then I saw them. They were sitting on the grass bank above the creek, his arms were round her and they were kissing like mad. So that they wouldn't see me I took a big circle by the footpath that runs behind the last of the houses.

It brought me out on the Woodside Road not far above where it joins the shore road. I got a fright when I passed a parked car, I thought it was empty, then I saw there was a couple necking like nobody's business. They didn't even look up when I passed, though they must have heard me. What a load of crap this sex business is!

Anyway, I got to the shore road again and nipped across a few yards further down. I got behind a rock and just kind of folded up. I thought I was going to *die,* it was so hard to breathe. But gradually it got easier, so I poked my head round the rock. They were quite a bit away but the glow in the sky showed them up as clear as day. He had his hand inside her anorak now, it was *disgusting*.

Funny thing, I never had any doubt I'd get Anne alone. I just had to wait and my chance would come.

So I waited.

PROLOGUE TO PART IV

"No, Willie!" Anne knew exactly how far she would let him go. She was entirely in control of the situation, as she was of most situations. Cool and relaxed, that was her line, and it came effortlessly, it wasn't a pose.

She'd discussed necking with Elma often enough, and Elma was full of practical advice. But Anne scarcely felt the need of advice, she had an instinctive grasp of such matters and her instinct seldom let her down. Even in her schoolwork she relied more on flair than on hard slogging: she could look at a complicated problem in geometry and *see* the answer before the rest of the class had understood the question.

So she could cope with Willie Toshak. He was a bit of a disappointment—clumsy and fumbling and . . . well, he *bored* her.

She liked boys, she'd enjoyed holding hands with Willie, she'd enjoyed kissing him. But that was enough. She didn't want to become *involved.* Not yet. Not with Willie Toshak.

He pulled his hand away from beneath her anorak. "Well, if *that's* how you feel about it," he said, sulking.

He took a crumpled pack of cigarettes from his pocket, put one in his mouth and lit it.

"Of course, I should have known," he said. "They warned me not to go out with a kid. You don't even smoke!"

Anne didn't answer.

After a bit he said truculently: "Well, what are you brooding about?"

"Celia."

"Celia! Why for God's sake?"

"She saw us tonight, Willie."

"Well, so what? She's a nutcase."

Yes, she was, in a way. But that didn't ease Anne's conscience.

It was a rotten thing they'd done, sneaking off while she wasn't looking. While she *was* looking, as it turned out, which made it worse.

Sure, Celia was a menace, she'd battened on Anne. A few kind words and she was clinging like a leech. This was always the trouble—people took *advantage* when you were nice to them. And then you couldn't shake them off.

Anne knew she would have to deal with Celia, make a clean break. But she always jibbed at the last moment, not wanting to hurt her. Celia was a pathetic creature really, with no other friends at all—unless you counted Helen Potts and Freda Landy.

"I hope she got home all right," Anne said.

"For heaven's sake, who *cares?*"

"I care."

He made a gesture of disgust. "I suppose you'll want me to take *you* home now?"

"Not if it's a burden to you." She was becoming very tired of Willie Toshak.

He nicked his cigarette and put the butt back in the packet. "Come on, then," he said gruffly and set off up the road.

Anne didn't follow. When he'd gone ten yards, he stopped. "Are you coming or not?" he called.

"No, thank you."

He turned away and trudged stolidly up the road towards the glow in the sky above the pier. He didn't look back again.

Anne sat on. She was a fool, she knew, but there was a streak of independence in her that refused to let her run after him. How dare he sulk, just because he didn't get his way!

She shivered. It had turned colder. Or perhaps the shiver came from the recollection of that night last summer when she and Lesley and Pat set off to cycle home and left Jan Allen here. Almost on this very spot.

Anne looked round. In front was the road, behind her the rocky track down to the beach. In this eerie light some of the rocks could look disturbingly human, but they were only rocks.

She was aware that she was at special risk. It wasn't only her age, there was her relationship with the other victims. Janice, Lesley and Anne: the triumvirate, Lesley had called them (trust Lesley to dredge up such a word)! And the last of these was Anne. Only yesterday Peeping Tom Baines had summed it up: "I've lost two of my best pupils, Miss Ridley: do take care of yourself. I'd hate to see the third go."

Yes, she was aware of her danger. Three green bottles, standing in a row. And yet, unbelievably, she'd allowed herself to be stranded here alone, late at night. Just to spite Willie Toshak.

The glow from the bonfire was dimming, the explosion of fireworks was more sporadic.

Anne stood up, had a last careful look round, then crossed to the road. She was frightened but not in a panic.

The headlights of a car were approaching from Moorend. Anne stood on the verge as it swept past.

She watched the rear lights disappear towards Chalford. For perhaps five seconds her thoughts were on the car and she forgot the danger from behind.

It was enough. The first warning she had was a gasping breath at her ear. Before she could even turn round, the hands were at her throat and she was fighting for her life.

Two things happened almost simultaneously. The grip on her neck slackened and a voice shouted, "Celia!" She passed out.

PART IV

MARK KENDALL

CHAPTER I

From an early age my heart was set on being a doctor, and the glamour of other careers never deflected me from that ambition. My brother Terry drifted into medicine, I consciously chose it.

Initially it was the simple urge to be like my father. He was so obviously a man of importance in the world, people went in awe of him. And he accepted it as his due, all that deference: he considered himself above the common herd.

He was a good doctor, my father, some said the best orthopaedic surgeon in London. A just man, too. But he lacked the common touch, there was no lightness in him, no humour. If Mandy thinks me pompous—well, there was my model. I've tried to cultivate humility, but we're all prisoners of the past.

My father took it as axiomatic that my career would parallel his, that I would end up as a consultant, or perhaps in a Chair in one of the big medical schools. I wasn't so confident; but even I had never expected to work in a second-rate general practice in a third-rate town in the north of England.

A shocking waste, my father would have said. I'm not so sure. True, the laboratory and X-ray services are primitive by the standards I'm used to, and Chalford Infirmary is straight out of Dickens. But these handicaps present a challenge. I've enjoyed the work.

Or would have, but for this damned cloud hanging over everything. I took the job in the first place because I wasn't satisfied about Terry's death. Mandy thinks it's arrogant of me to criticise the police and try to do their job for them. But, really, their record is appalling. I still believe Lesley Peterson would be alive today if they'd heeded my warning.

They've no sense of urgency, you'd think time was on their side. Superintendent Egmont said yesterday on the radio that they've interviewed over fifty thousand people in the last two weeks and a computer's now digesting the answers. And meanwhile a time bomb's ticking away. . . .

There's going to be another killing, I feel it in my bones. I said so to John Armitage this morning.

He's a funny chap, Armitage, he's so terrified of becoming involved that you sometimes wonder if he *exists*. I used to think he was just lazy. Well, he *is* lazy, but it's more than that. He's highly intelligent, yet outside of his work you'll never get him to express an opinion on anything. Not on *anything*.

So all he said today was: "Another killing? Don't say that to Gwen, it would only upset her." Then he asked me to call on a patient at Moorend. A private patient. But of course I won't get the fee.

It stands to reason there'll be another murder. The man is insane and a sadist, he'll not stop killing until he's caught.

"So what would you do about it?" Shelagh asked me the other evening. Like Mandy, she thinks I'm obsessed with the case.

"I shouldn't waste time questioning everyone in Chalford. I'd stick to the ones at the dinner party the night Terry was murdered."

"But, darling, it's so unlike you to jump to conclusions like that."

Darling? We were getting on, it seemed. . . .

Was I jumping to conclusions? I still didn't see how the murderer could have known he would find Terry on the cliff path so late that night unless he heard the appointment being made.

There was more than that, though. At the back of my mind was the shadow of a recollection—something I'd seen, perhaps, or a remark I'd heard—that made me certain the killer was someone I knew, someone I knew well. If I let it simmer for a while, the shadow would become substance. . . .

Remember, remember the fifth of November.

The tradition was strong in Chalford, they made a meal of it. It wasn't just groups of kids burning their effigies and letting off a few fireworks: there was a set piece on the beach, with torch-light procession, bonfire, the lot.

It should have been cancelled this year, it was an open invitation to the murderer. People protested and there were letters to the local paper, but all in vain. The Town Council decided to go ahead on the theory that the children were safer concentrated in one area than scattered over the town.

I pointed out to Detective Inspector Robens that they would be safer still at home.

"You can't stop the kids enjoying themselves," he said. "Anyway, we'll have extra men on duty."

That's what they all said: you couldn't expect children to stay home on Guy Fawkes Night. The police would protect them.

Just as they had protected Janice Allen and Lesley Peterson. . . .

Even Gwen Armitage was persuaded to let Celia go out. The snob appeal of a party at the Richardses' did the trick (Harry Richards is managing director of the shipyard). Mandy was detailed to keep an eye on her.

They've a hell of a nerve asking Mandy to do *anything* for them, considering the way they treat her. But she didn't object. I think she felt, like me, that the strangler might be abroad that night; and Celia was in the front line.

I'd hoped it would pour with rain, to dampen the enthusiasm and keep some of the kids at home. But of course it didn't: the weather was sharp, clear, windless. Ideal for pyrotechnics.

I was on duty at Vine Street in the evening. There was a thinnish attendance and I was through soon after eight.

I crossed to the Greyhound and had my usual sandwich and pint; I rarely bothered to go home for a meal after the Vine Street surgery.

More often than not Shelagh Carey would join me in the pub

and afterwards we'd go for a stroll or a run in the car and usually end up at her place for coffee. It was all very casual, no commitment on either side. We couldn't go on like this, the relationship had to develop or break, the issue couldn't be shirked indefinitely. Once or twice, as I kissed her good night, I knew this was the girl for me, and nearly told her so.

But I didn't. Something made me hold back. If this was love, it was not the way I'd felt about Zelda. None the worse for that, I suppose. And yet . . .

By half-past eight tonight Shelagh still wasn't there. She hadn't *promised*, of course, it wasn't a firm date. But usually she told me if she wasn't going to make it.

I missed her. She was a good listener, Shelagh, a person I liked to be with at the end of a hard day. It was relaxing just to look at her gorgeous big eyes and the understanding smile. I'd never heard her being bitchy about anyone, not even about Mandy, who gave her plenty of cause. When Shelagh came for a meal to Tramore Avenue, Mandy was *insufferably* rude. It made me angry.

By a quarter to nine I realised Shelagh wasn't coming. The evening stretched emptily ahead.

I thought of going round to her flat, but that was too positive a step, it would upset the delicate balance of our relationship and start a new phase which I didn't want to start yet.

So I drove idly down towards the pier, attracted by the flickering lights of the torches. I parked on the promenade, crossed to the railing and joined the crowd looking down at the scene below.

The last of the procession had just arrived on the sands and was completing the deep ring of lights round the big black mound that was to be the pyre. There was scarcely a sound apart from the swoosh and suck of the waves on the beach.

As I watched, a small figure detached itself from the circle and ran back up the sands towards the steps lending to the road. Almost at once another—adult—figure followed. Also running.

The second was a woman. And there was something familiar about the way she moved. It was Mandy Armitage, I was sure of it. Which meant that the child was Celia.

I went back to my car, drove along as far as the steps, then turned up towards the town. I caught up on Mandy at the intersection before High Street.

I stopped at the red light, opened the nearside door, and called her name. She looked at me in disbelief, hesitated, then climbed in.

The lights changed to green, I put the car in gear, we crossed and started the climb towards High Street.

"Pull into the side," Mandy said sharply.

"What?"

"Stop the car!"

I braked and stopped by the kerb.

"Put off your headlights."

I switched them off. "Anything else?" I said.

"Look!" She pointed ahead, towards the lights of High Street. At the corner was a girl, almost bent double in a paroxysm of coughing. Her back was towards us.

"Is it Celia?" I said.

"Yes."

"Well, hadn't we better—"

"She'll be all right. She's been running too fast, that's all."

"I think we should take her home."

"No, Mark!"

I looked at her: she was white and tense. "What's going on, Mandy?"

"I wish to God I knew," she said. "If you'd seen her face, it was *evil*. . . ."

Celia had straightened, but was still panting. She never looked in our direction.

As we sat there, the sky behind was suffused in a yellow glow. The bonfire had been lit. We could faintly hear shouting and laughter, then came renewed explosions of rockets and fireworks.

Celia began walking east down High Street.

"She's not going home," I said.

"I think she's looking for Anne Ridley. Follow her, Mark, but keep well back." Mandy was jumpy as a cat, her voice shaky.

We drove up to the corner and turned right. Celia was fifty yards away, walking fast.

I stopped the car. At this distance she would recognise us if she turned round.

"Tell me about it, Mandy," I said. "What are you afraid of?"

She didn't answer directly. "Celia heard that phone call," she said.

"What?"

"At the dinner party. The night your brother died. Celia answered the phone, she would know Terry was to be out on that cliff—"

"Good God, Mandy, you can't be serious! *Celia!* She's only a *child.* . . ."

"A child with the strength of an adult. Start up now, Mark."

We hugged the pavement, just keeping Celia in sight. She had started to run again. She seemed in no doubt where she was going.

Mandy said: "She's always *loathed* these three—Janice, Lesley and Anne. It's Gwen's fault, really. She kept trying to buy their friendship for Celia, and they snubbed her again and again. Janice and Lesley did, anyway. Anne was friendlier, but she ditched Celia tonight. That's why she's so mad."

I was still sceptical. I couldn't accept a thirteen-year-old girl, however strong, as the strangler.

"She's been out every time it happened," Mandy said. "Had you noticed that?"

"Even the night Terry died?"

"Well, she *could* have slipped out that night—nobody checked to see if she was in bed. . . . But the damning thing, Mark, is the lie she told about Lesley's death."

Celia turned right, off High Street, down Shoreditch Lane. "I think she's making for Abbot's Creek," I said.

"I'm sure of it. That's where Anne and her boy friend will be. Go round the long way."

I accelerated, and we took a wide sweep round by Woodside estate. We should still get to the creek before Celia.

"What do you mean?" I said. "What lie?"

"About the man she saw in Piper Lane. She described him down to the colour of his tie, almost. She couldn't possibly have seen so much—the light's so bad you could hardly distinguish between male and female at that distance."

"Well, all right, she's untruthful, we know that. She wanted a bit of notoriety, that's all. So she made the story up."

"But she did see the *car*. She described the exact spot where it was parked, and Anne Ridley confirmed it. Celia's scared, Mark, she goes wild when you question her about that night. I've tried."

"So you assume she's a murderer?"

"I don't assume it. I fear it. She's . . . never been *normal*, you know. . . . Put your lights off now. And the engine."

We coasted down towards the bay and stopped under a tree just short of the junction with the coast road.

"There they are," Mandy said. Sitting on a grassy mound beyond the road, perhaps fifty yards west of the junction, were a young couple in a clinch, their figures etched against the brilliant skyline.

"That's Anne Ridley, is it?" I asked.

"Yes."

"And the boy?"

"Willie Toshak."

"So what now?"

"We wait."

A minute or two passed. Then, without warning, Mandy's arms were round me and she pulled my head down.

"Mandy, for God's sake—"

"Sh!"

Then I heard the tiptoeing footsteps. They paused just outside the car and there was the sound of harsh, laboured breathing, then the footsteps continued down towards the beach.

Mandy released me and I sat up. Celia was turning left at the corner. She disappeared from view.

"She'll cross lower down where they can't see her," Mandy said. "Lucky she didn't recognise the car."

"Look, that girl's ill, Mandy. It's time we put a stop to this and took her home."

"No. We must find out what she's up to."

"But—"

"Mark, we *must*."

So we sat in the car and waited. And all the time rockets were bursting in the sky and scattering red and green and yellow stars.

Once I thought I detected a movement among the boulders across from where we sat. But it could have been a trick of the light.

The lovers' clinch had broken, and the boy was smoking a cigarette. When I wound down my window, I could hear their voices. They were quarrelling.

Presently the boy set off up the road towards the town. He stopped, expecting the girl to follow. But she didn't. So he carried on and disappeared into the night.

"My God, she's a *fool*," Mandy muttered. She opened the door at her side. "Don't follow me," she said. "Just keep watching, and be ready." She went back up the Woodside Road and joined the footpath which circles the row of houses there. I guessed she was working her way round to the coast road.

Anne was still sitting on the same spot. But now she stood up, looked all round several times, as if apprehensive. As well she might be.

I had my door open, ready to intervene if needed. I still couldn't believe that Celia Armitage represented a serious threat. But it was eerie all the same to think of her lurking down there somewhere among the rocks.

Anne moved forward to the road. A car was approaching from Moorend and she stopped on the verge to let it pass.

Everything happened in a flash. A second figure appeared from behind, Anne gave a strangled scream, then she was struggling on the ground with the other on top, and I was running, and Mandy yelled, "Celia!"

It was all over in seconds. The girl was scarcely hurt, she'd fainted from sheer fright. Celia's breath was coming in great, deep shudders; and Mandy was staring at her in horror.

I went back and brought the car round. There were two hospital cases here by the look of it.

When I returned, Anne had come round and Mandy was comforting her. Celia was still sobbing and shuddering.

I got them into the car, Celia beside me in the front, the other two in the back.

Nobody had said anything yet about what happened. But now Celia wailed: "I only meant to give her a fright."

"Don't talk just now," I said, starting the engine.

"You certainly managed it," Anne said shakily. "I thought I'd had it."

Mandy said: "You would have, if we hadn't been there."

"Oh no, Miss Armitage, Celia was only kidding. She took her hands off *before* you yelled. I remember it clearly. It was just before I fainted."

It was a magnanimous statement. Was it true? I thought so. But Mandy shut up tight.

I didn't like the way Celia was breathing. She kept moaning and calling for Uncle Ben.

It's a curious thing, but Ben Radford, whom I would hardly trust to bandage a cut finger, is quite wonderful with Celia Armitage. I had no compunction in ringing for him when we got to the hospital.

He was round in five minutes. The nurses had her in bed by this time, but she was still hysterical.

"What the hell happened?" Radford said. He looked under the weather himself and I smelt alcohol from his breath.

I explained briefly. "I haven't given her anything," I said. "You'll know what she's on."

He nodded. "Leave her to me, Mark. Does Gwen know?"

"Yes." I'd phoned her also.

Anne had more or less recovered; she was a resilient child. We drove her home, Mandy and I.

Anne said: "Don't be too hard on Celia, please. She was just jealous tonight, and it was my fault—I was mean to her."

Mandy said nothing. So Anne continued: "You're not going to report this, are you? I mean, to the police or anything?"

"We'll think about it, Anne," I said.

"Well, I'm not going to mention it, that's for sure."

We dropped Anne at her house and started back. Mandy still hadn't uttered.

"I'm sure you're wrong, Mandy," I said.

"I don't want to talk about it."

"Apart from anything else, Celia couldn't have driven a car. Remember in Lesley's diary—"

"I said I don't want to talk about it."

I looked at her and saw she was crying. I stopped the car.

"I'm sorry, Mandy. This must have been a strain for you."

"A strain!" She gave a bitter laugh. "You did this, Mark, it's all your fault."

"*My* fault?"

"You're so positive the murderer's someone we know, someone at that dinner party. One of my family or one of their friends. And I end up suspecting my own sister!"

"But you don't any longer, do you?"

"No, of course not. I got carried away when I thought about the motive: why were *particular* girls—Janice and Lesley—picked out? And then I remembered that Celia hated them both. And the third girl she was jealous of was Anne Ridley. . . . Poor Celia! What a rotten, suspicious nature I've got!"

She sniffed. There were tears running down her cheeks. I gave her a handkerchief.

Without her glasses she looked very young and appealing. I'd rather enjoyed that pantomime at Abbot's Creek when she put her arms round me. I was tempted to try a second showing.

But I refrained. She was not the kind of girl to take liberties with.

So we set off for home, silent again. I was depressed. The evening had ended in anti-climax, which ought to have pleased me. It didn't, and I couldn't think why.

At the east end of High Street we were stopped by the police. They'd set up a road block.

A constable shone his torch on Mandy, then flashed it over the empty back seat.

"May I see in the boot, sir?"

I got out and opened it.

"Thank you, sir," the constable said after a quick examination.

"What's this in aid of?" I asked. But I think I knew already.

"A schoolgirl's missing," he said. "She hasn't come back from the bonfire."

"If it's Anne Ridley, we've just taken her home."

"No, that wasn't the name, sir."

"Then who?"

He hesitated, then shone the torch in my face. "It's Dr. Kendall, isn't it?"

"Yes."

"I believe her name is Richards, sir. Pat Richards."

CHAPTER 2

The body wasn't on the golf course this time. They found it under a hedge in her own garden. Naked, like the others. Strangled, like the others.

She'd been dead, the pathologist said, since about nine o'clock. Which meant she'd never been to the beach at all, she must have been murdered soon after the party in her garden broke up.

Celia Armitage and Anne Ridley both said that Pat had come out of the gate with them, carrying her torch. They were the last to leave.

They hadn't gone far when someone called Pat back. Both Celia and Anne heard *something*, but weren't sure what—not even whether it was a man's voice or a woman's.

Pat had heard, though. "I'm wanted," she said. "Just go on— I'll catch up." The others assumed it was her father or mother with some last-minute instruction. They never saw her again.

Most of this didn't become generally known until the inquest. But we got Celia's version almost right away.

She came home from hospital in triumph after only one night, pale, but in fair shape. Ben Radford, had, as usual, done his witch-doctoring well. Or perhaps it was Pat Richards' death that worked the oracle. Celia drew strength from others' misfortunes.

She herself was now cleared, for her alibi was cast iron: she'd been with Anne in the torchlight procession, and afterwards Mandy and I followed her to Abbot's Creek.

The public outcry in Chalford was immediate and violent. A mass meeting of parents and teachers was followed by a protest march on the police station. Nor was the indignation confined to Chalford. The "Nude Stranglings" were now a national issue, questions were asked in Parliament.

But the police seemed unmoved by the pressure, and the investigation continued at its painstaking pace.

I had a session with Detective Inspector Robens, who looked so grey and defeated I almost felt sorry for him.

I gave him an account of Celia's attack on Anne Ridley. He nodded as if he'd heard it all before.

He said: "Did you know this girl Richards?"

"Only by sight."

"A bit different from the other two, wouldn't you say?"

I knew what he meant: Pat Richards didn't fit the pattern. Janice and Lesley had been pretty girls, and exceptionally intelligent, whereas Pat was small and scrawny and below average in the class. Besides, she was only on the fringe of the group that Janice, Lesley and Anne had dominated.

Inspector Robens lit a cigarette and began to cough.

"Did you ever discover," I asked him, "who sent that note? The one that said Terry was *pushed* over the cliff?"

His cough continued longer than was clinically necessary. It was like John Armitage's wheeze, that cough: a defensive weapon. Finally he said: "Matter of fact, we did."

"Who was it?"

"We may not take the Hippocratic oath, Dr. Kendall, but there are things we keep to ourselves."

"It was Terry's mistress, wasn't it?"

Instead of answering, he returned to last Friday. "You were on duty at Vine Street, you said? What time?"

"From seven till about eight-fifteen."

"You didn't come home afterwards?"

"No."

"So you don't know what the other members of the household were doing?"

"Dr. Armitage was on evening surgery *here*, with Dr. Cohen. Six o'clock till seven as a rule. What he did afterwards I've no idea."

"And Mrs. Armitage?"

"She was at home when I rang from the hospital. But that was nearly eleven o'clock."

"And Mandy was chaperoning her stepsister?"

"Yes."

"Of course, we don't know when she joined her. Celia never actually *saw* her."

The insinuation unreasonably annoyed me. I said: "You're asking these questions about two murders too late."

He coughed again. I longed to tell him he was digging his grave.

He said: "We couldn't drop everything, sir, just because *you* had a hunch. But we did make a special study of your short list."

"The dinner guests?"

"Yes."

"And?"

"It's not been easy. Three of them live alone"—he meant Radford, Baines and Shelagh Carey—"and have no one to vouch for them. As for the Armitages, their lives are in separate compartments, none of them ever knows where the others are." Or cares, he might have added.

"I'm telling you all this," he went on (all what? He'd told me practically nothing), "because I need your help." Cough, cough, cough. The signal for another cigarette. "You've lived in this house for six weeks, Dr. Kendall, you were around when the last two deaths took place. You know all six people who were here the night your brother died—"

"Six? There were *eight*, not counting Terry."

"Dr. and Mrs. Cohen were in Scotland at the time the first murder was committed. We can forget them."

True. "All right, I know the six."

"You claim one of them did it, and you could be right. But *which?*"

"I don't know."

"The killer is insane. You'd accept that?"

"Yes."

"Well, wouldn't there be some *sign* of mental disturbance?"

"Not necessarily. Schizos can appear terrifyingly sane to their families and friends."

"Yes, but to a doctor? Haven't *you* noticed any tell-tale sign?"

"No, I haven't."

Superficial oddities of behaviour tell nothing: we're all off centre, there's no such thing as the average man. Or woman.

Of the six only Shelagh Carey was without obvious eccentricities. All the others—even Mandy—had their sharp edges. But it wasn't significant.

Inspector Robens said: "Do you ever discuss the murders with them?"

"In Chalford it's hard to discuss anything else these days."

"You see, that kind of criminal usually likes to *talk* about it. And he'd be more relaxed with you than with us. He might make a slip, he might say too much. Bear that in mind, will you?"

It was, I suppose, an olive branch. I said I would bear it in mind.

He was coughing again as he left me.

On Tuesday I had my first stint at Vine Street since Guy Fawkes Night.

This time Shelagh was waiting in the Greyhound. We had a drink together, then went for a run. The weather had broken and a fine drizzle was falling.

We went over the hill to Moorend and back by the coast road. I was driving as a kind of therapy, hardly noticing which way we went. I'd been called out of bed twice the previous night and was tired.

She's quick, Shelagh, to sense when you don't want to talk. She never *chatters*.

I stopped at Abbot's Creek.

Shelagh said: "This is where Celia attacked Anne Ridley, isn't it?"

"Yes."

It all began at Abbot's Creek, I was reflecting. It all began that summer evening when three girls rode off on their bicycles and left a fourth here alone.

"How did he know Janice would be here?" I said.

"Who?"

"The murderer. No one could have foreseen she'd be walking home alone."

"*I* knew. I drove her down to the creek."

True. But no one else was likely to know. Which suggested that the murderer just happened to be passing, and was tempted. . . .

Passing? On foot? No, surely by car. The three girls on their bikes saw Terry walking down the edge of the golf course towards the stile. He climbed over it onto the road, but didn't see Janice. However, he did see *something* that bothered him afterwards. Mandy believed he'd recognised someone's car.

Whose car? Well, if the murder wasn't planned, the car hadn't gone there just to pick Janice up. So where had it been, where was it going?

Abbot's Creek was at the extreme end of Chalford. There was only the coast road to Moorend, five miles away, and the ring road via the Woodside estate.

Which meant you wouldn't pass the creek except to enter or leave the town. So the murderer must have had some reason for going out of Chalford that evening.

Well, there were plausible reasons. Mandy had her voluntary hospital work in Moorend, John Armitage and Ben Radford had country patients to visit.

In fact, by his own admission, Armitage *had* passed the creek and *had* seen Janice.

"What's the matter, Mark?" Shelagh had been sitting so quietly I'd almost forgotten she was there.

"Just a passing thought. Let's go."

But instead of driving home I took the twisting road that climbs the hill to the golf clubhouse. There were patches of mist up here; the lights of the town below us winked fitfully.

At the intersection fifty yards short of the clubhouse I turned right. There was a scrunch of tyres on gravel.

I said: "This is where John Armitage saw the car on the night Lesley died."

"Are you doing a reconstruction or something?"

"That's the general idea."

The road was narrow, and rutted in places, and the gradient steep. I crawled down in second gear. After half a mile the track petered out as it debouched on a grassy hollow. On the left was the golf course, above and on the right the footpath along the cliff.

I turned the car to face the ninth fairway, switched off the engine and the lights. The only sound now was the patter of rain on the windscreen. Until our eyes became attuned, it seemed totally dark.

Shelagh snuggled up close and put her head on my shoulder. "I'm *scared*," she said.

She didn't sound very scared. But I put my arm round her and she sighed contentedly.

But my mind was busy. Two murders had been committed here, a third only just frustrated. And over there, two hundred yards away, at the Devil's Shoulder, a third murder *had* been done.

Almost on this very spot Lesley Peterson had sat in fear of her life. Until Terry appeared in the nick of time.

It was only a reprieve. What had Lesley felt that second time, when there was no Terry to save her? Did she know she was going to be strangled like Janice before her?

"Any inspiration?" Shelagh asked, her voice muffled.

"None."

"Well, forget it, Mark. It's not very complimentary to me." She was giggling.

"Why did he strip them?" I said.

"I'm told men enjoy seeing naked girls."

"Yes, but—" I let it drop. Even Shelagh was losing patience.

I kissed her. She responded warmly, and I got carried away. Perhaps it was the setting: we were alone in this little island of warmth, sealed off from the hostile elements outside. I remember saying, "I love you, Shelagh," and hearing her contented murmur.

And then, somehow, we were discussing wedding plans. Shelagh was warm and happy and loving.

And so was I. Until, out of the blue, there came to me a picture —not of Zelda, that would have been understandable—but of Mandy Armitage's tear-stained face in this same car last Friday. And in some curious way I felt I had betrayed her.

"It's getting late," I said. "We'd better go."

"Must we? All right." She released me, sat up straight, buttoned her blouse, put her suede jacket over her shoulders. "I'm just *dying* to tell people. Aren't you?"

"Yes," I said, switching on the engine.

As I reversed in a rapid arc the headlights on full beam picked out the big wooden shed.

"Poor Terry!" Shelagh said. Like an epitaph.

"What?"

"I was remembering how he used to come here to meet Meg. . . . I couldn't give him what he wanted."

"He was hard to please," I said dutifully.

"No, it was my fault." I don't believe in intercourse before marriage—I'm not proud of it, it's just how I was brought up."

As I nosed the car up the narrow road between the hedges, I was remembering one of Terry's last letters. *Surely* that had implied that he and Shelagh—

My God, this was terrible! Ten minutes engaged, and already I was doubting her!

I said: "Who was Meg, Shelagh?"

"A tart, a whore, a prostitute—choose your term."

"You don't know her surname?"

"No." She giggled. "I do know one other thing about her."

"What's that?"

"She's plump. Terry used to say I wasn't so well-covered as Meg. . . . And I'm no skeleton, am I?"

"No, you're not. . . . I'd like to talk to her."

"What about?"

"Terry's death. She sent that note. She must have seen Terry being pushed over the cliff."

"Haven't the police traced her, then?"

"Yes, but they won't tell me who she is."

"Well, her evidence can't have been worth much."

"I'd still like to know what it was."

Shelagh yawned. "We could always knock on every door in Chalford and ask if fat Meg lives here. . . ."

CHAPTER 3

Breakfast at the Armitages' was a scrappy meal. Gwen, who never took any herself, drifted about in a house-coat, Mandy had her coffee by the hall telephone, John rarely appeared until after we were all finished. Which left Celia and me at the table.

You couldn't carry on a normal conversation with Celia. I rarely tried. And I certainly wasn't going to give her the first news of my engagement.

When I finished breakfast, Mandy was on the phone and Gwen nowhere to be seen. So I put off saying anything till lunch.

Ben Radford was lunching with us that day (as he often did) and arrived with a bottle of sherry—"as a celebration," he explained to Gwen.

"Of what?"

"Why, of Mark's engagement, of course."

Shelagh must have wasted no time in spreading the news. I guessed that Tom Baines had told Ben. Not that it mattered, I didn't give a damn if the Armitages were offended. Except that I'd wanted to break the news myself to Mandy, to *explain* to her.

To explain what? That I was in love with another girl? Why should she be interested? Although she'd defrosted a little recently, her attitude to me was still cool.

She made the conventional responses now, congratulated me, drank our health. But all in that brittle, off-hand manner she cultivated.

Gwen herself, once she'd got over her initial pique, was enthusiastic. "We must have a proper celebration," she said. "A small dinner party. How about Saturday? Just you and Shelagh, Mark, and the three partners, of course. And perhaps you could bring a friend, Mandy."

"I haven't any friends," Mandy said, staring at me.

"Nonsense, dear! What about that nice young man at Shelagh's school? Tom Baines, I mean."

The remark was offensive, she must have known how Mandy despised Baines. Baiting her stepdaughter was Gwen's favourite sport.

Mandy said: "Invite him if you like, Gwen, but he's probably got a date with a boy friend."

Ben Radford spluttered and started to protest. He's a great splutterer, Ben.

Just then Celia arrived home for lunch, bursting with the news that was already all round school.

"Is it true?" she asked me.

"Yes."

"Gosh, I hope *you* don't get pushed over a cliff!" And she laughed. As always, more shrilly than the remark justified. Then she said to Mandy: "That leaves you on the shelf again, eh?" Another laugh.

Mandy said nothing. Gwen smiled indulgently.

As for John Armitage, he had scarcely spoken since Ben arrived. He just stood there with his sherry glass, gazing benignly into space.

What did he think of Celia? Or Mandy? Or my engagement to Shelagh Carey? Impossible to say.

Ben Radford and I were on evening surgery at Tramore Avenue. My last patient had just left when Ben looked in.

"Mandy told me you were still here," he said. "I never really got a chance this morning to say how delighted I am. Shelagh's an exceptionally nice girl."

"Thanks, Ben."

He carefully closed the door. "Celia wasn't so far wrong about Mandy, you know: she's fallen for you."

"Oh, come off it! She can't stand me."

He shook his head. "A complex character, Mandy. You only see the tip of the iceberg. . . . No, iceberg's the wrong metaphor. She can be a spitfire, but it's all bottled up. Not at all a comfortable person."

The remark annoyed me. "It's hardly surprising, considering how they treat her at home. If I'd been Celia's father, I'd have boxed her ears for that remark to Mandy today."

"Can you imagine John Armitage doing anything so positive?"

"No. Frankly, I don't understand that man."

"Pleasure is the absence of pain—that's his philosophy. If you don't become involved, you don't get hurt."

Ben Radford could be quite shrewd in his judgments. It was only when you pricked the bubble by asking him to *do* something that you discovered his inadequacy.

He was sitting on the examination couch filling his pipe. "Of course," he said, "John wasn't always like that."

"Wasn't he?"

"Oh no! When I came here first, he was a *dynamo*. A damn good doctor—"

"He still is."

"Yes, but he hasn't the *dedication* now." (It was ironical to hear Ben Radford speak of dedication.) "They had quite a social life, too, he and Gwen. You'd never guess it now."

No, but I'd heard about it. I'd also heard hints of the scandal that changed everything.

"What went wrong?" I asked, pretending ignorance.

"Their child for a start. Celia was two years old when I joined the practice, and already there were signs that she was—well, *backward*. There's not much wrong with her. Given good health, she'd have got by. But she was sickly as well, she needed constant attention."

"And got too much?"

"You mean she was spoiled? Perhaps. It wasn't easy. Gwen refused to face the facts. Her child was normal, she maintained, the only problem was to cure the asthma. John saw the truth all

right and deep down I think it hurt him even more. . . . The
point is, no one loved Celia for what she was." He stopped to light
his pipe. "Unless you count me."

I tried again. "You said 'their child for a start.' What *else*
went wrong?"

"Well, you see, Gwen had me dancing attendance on Celia.
Hardly a day passed but she called me in on one pretext or
another. She was obsessed with motherhood, she could talk by
the hour about nappy rash and potty training and whatever. . . .
And dammit, I had to listen, I was the young assistant with
ambitions for a partnership."

"So tongues wagged?" A female patient, elderly and indiscreet,
had told me this before I could stop her.

"Well, you know what people are," Ben said. "They sniff sex
behind every closed door. It was laughable, really, because, as you
know, I'm not a great lady's man."

The oddly spinsterish expression made me wonder again about
his friendship with Tom Baines.

"But John Armitage believed the rumours?" I said.

"Yes. He had a hell of a row with Gwen one night and—well,
they made a deal. I was to stay on and get a partnership provided
I moved out of Tramore Avenue. For a long time I wasn't allowed
in the house, except professionally when Celia was ill."

"John and Gwen fixed this without consulting you?"

"John announced it next day."

"What reason did he give?"

"None. We never discussed the reason."

"And you didn't *ask?*"

"I didn't need to—Gwen had given me all the information.
She'd confessed to sleeping with me, even though it wasn't true.
She was tired of sharing a bed with John, she made her *own*
package deal: they haven't shared a room since."

"And you let Armitage go on believing you'd been his wife's
lover?"

Ben shrugged. "It suited me. I got a partnership out of it." And
when I continued to stare: "Dammit, it's easy for you, Mark, the

world's at your feet. I'm run-of-the-mill and I was damn glad to be made a partner so soon."

It made sense. Perhaps also, if he really was a homosexual, the rumour linking his name with Gwen's provided useful cover.

Gwen's motive was less easy to divine. I asked Ben about it.

"I told you: she'd gone off John, couldn't bear him to touch her. She blamed him for Celia's defects, both the asthma and the one she wouldn't admit to. You must understand, Mark, Gwen's whole life is centred on her daughter. She's unbalanced about it."

"Why didn't John divorce her?"

"He hates scandal, that's why. It would have *humiliated* him to cite me as corespondent. So he grins and bears it. Or at any rate he bears it. But don't imagine he's *happy* about the situation. It was a very unhealthy atmosphere for Celia to grow up in."

"And for Mandy."

"Mandy? She's got an inner strength, she'll not crack. But Celia has nothing. And no one."

"Except you."

"Yes, except me. I'm very fond of her, always have been. Of course, I like children. Before they grow up and the *rot* sets in." He looked at his watch. "You'll not be popular with Gwen if you let your supper get cold."

I said: "Ben, did Terry talk to you much?"

"What about?"

"Well, *anything.*"

"Not really. He was a moody character, your brother. And anyway he preferred *female* company."

"That's just the point. You know he used to meet a girl when he took the dog out at nights?"

"So I've heard." He said it almost primly.

"You've no idea who the girl was?"

"Terry would never have discussed that with me."

No, if Mandy didn't know, and Shelagh, Ben Radford was a long shot.

But he added: "I'll tell you who *might* know."

"Who?"

"Tom Baines. He was a buddy of Terry's." I hadn't heard the word "buddy" since I'd been in the States.

I rang Baines after supper and invited him to the Greyhound for a drink. He was there before me and his nose was already in a pint of bitter. I carried over another for him.

"I hear we've to congratulate you," he greeted me.

"Thanks."

"I warned you she was the marrying type, remember?"

"It's not usually considered a fault."

"She'll run your life so smoothly you'll hardly hear the engine tick over. A wonderful wife. If that's what you want."

I decided not to take offence. I said: "I was half in love before we met, I'd heard so much about her from Terry."

"Well, one thing for sure, *that* would never have worked. She'd have smothered Terry."

"I'm not so sure. Terry was a psychological mess, Shelagh could have been the saving of him."

Baines shrugged. "I'm a psychological mess, too, so my opinion doesn't count. But Shelagh Carey makes me want to throw up. . . . However, let's not quarrel. You didn't ask me here for my assessment of your beloved."

"It's about Terry, as a matter of fact. Who was the girl he used to meet on the golf course?"

"Why should you want to know that?"

"Never mind why. Did you know her?"

"I met her once. I was having a jar with Terry—in this pub, as a matter of fact—when in she walked. She'd come to put off some date, and he was *furious*."

"Why?"

"Well, he said she should have phoned, he'd told her never to contact him here. Mandy Armitage might have been with him, you see. At that time Mandy used to wait for him here after his surgery. Just like you and Shelagh now."

He knew the score pretty well.

"What was she like?" I said.

"Meg? On the buxom side. Fairish hair, not much make-up,

quietly dressed—she didn't *look* a professional tart. And in fact she wasn't, not really. She was married, with a kid. Her husband had left her and she lived with her mother. So Terry told me."

"What's her name?"

"He just called her Meg."

"Nothing else you can remember?"

"'Fraid not. . . . No, wait. She had a job, he said. In a shop or something. A hairdressers', that was it."

"You're sure?"

"Yes. . . . What's all this in aid of, Mark?"

"I'm still looking for the man who pushed my brother over a cliff."

"Then I wish you luck. He's decimated my second-year history class."

He'd finished his second pint. "My turn," he said, and went over to the bar.

When he came back, he said: "Where's Shelagh tonight? I thought you'd be celebrating."

"She's breaking the news to her mother in Leeds. She couldn't wait till I was free to go with her."

"Well, well," Baines said, "Mother Carey will be well pleased with her chicken tonight."

It was becoming hard not to lose my temper. "If you're implying that Shelagh set out to trap me—"

He laughed. "Don't go all pompous on me, Mark. You're not president of the Royal College yet, you know." He lifted his glass. "Here's to lots of little Kendalls. . . . She's damn good with kids, I'll give her that," he added. "If they had a popularity poll at school, she'd run away with it. And they say children are sound judges of character!"

"Well, aren't they?"

"Good God, no! Flatter a child's vanity and you're his idol. I have my faults, Mark, but flattery's not one of them."

"These three girls who died, Tom—you taught them all?"

"Yes, I taught them all."

"What did you think of them?"

"The Richards girl was no loss to scholarship. The other two

—well, I'm not dedicated to my profession like your Shelagh, but we've few enough intelligent kids to teach without having some nut strangle them. These two were very bright. Damn good-looking, too. Especially little Janice. She'd nice legs, that girl." He grinned. "Don't look so puritan, Mark. If you had to spend your day cramming history into thick skulls, your eyes would stray to their legs occasionally. . . . They call me Peeping Tom, did you know that?"

"Yes."

"I think it's insulting, myself. I don't peep, I *stare.*"

"But you weren't interested in Pat Richards' legs?"

"God forbid! I don't collect matchsticks. Which makes me wonder why *she* was a victim. Seems to me it's been too readily assumed there's some perverted sex motive behind these murders."

"What other motive could there be?"

"Well, one asks oneself if there could be some link between the three victims—I mean, beyond the fact that they're all girls, they're all thirteen, they're all pupils of the same school."

"And have you found the missing link?"

"I'm not sure. I stumbled on one curious fact, which could be just coincidence. But if it *is* significant, then there's one more child, and only one, in danger.

"Stop talking in riddles, Tom. Which child?"

"Celia Armitage."

"Why?"

"My dear Mark, why don't you ask your fiancée? She too has access to the evidence."

CHAPTER 4

We had a scare on Thursday when Celia didn't come home for lunch. Such was the prevailing tension that Gwen was in tears and John rang the police.

It turned out she'd played truant from school to attend the inquest on Pat Richards.

"I never got to the others," she explained, when she finally came home. "I wasn't missing this one."

All her mother said was: "So long as you're *safe*, darling. . . ."

I told Shelagh about it. We were having dinner *à deux* in her flat to celebrate our engagement. Fillet steaks, a bottle of Nuits-St.-Georges, candlelight, flowers, soft music.

Shelagh said: "She's quite irresponsible, that child. She ought not to be mixing with ordinary children. It's not safe."

"Who for?"

She raised her eyebrows. "The others, of course. Look what she did to Anne Ridley last Friday. She might have killed her."

"Tom Baines believes Celia herself is in danger."

"How does he make that out?"

"Some odd fact he's dug up—he wouldn't say what. But he claims you know it, too."

"You shouldn't listen to Baines, darling: he doesn't like me."

"He must be unique." No, not quite: Mandy didn't like her either.

"Tom doesn't like women, fullstop," she added. "But enough of him. Mummy was thrilled to bits, Mark—she's *dying* to meet you."

"Good. We must arrange it soon." Why didn't I feel more eager?

Shelagh was moulded in a lilac-coloured midi dress. She'd just missed being beautiful, but made the most of the assets she had: her eyes, her glossy black hair, her figure.

"You never told me where you got your scar," I said.

"Oh that?" She felt her cheek. "My brother did that when he was six. He hadn't learned that a broken glass was a lethal weapon."

It was the first time she'd mentioned a brother. She was reticent about her family, slightly ashamed of them, I guessed.

After dinner we blew out the candles and made ourselves comfortable on a sofa in front of the fire. We talked intermittently and we kissed and it was all very agreeable; and all so different from those passionate sessions with Zelda last year. More civilised, I told myself.

"Who does your hair?" I asked. I loved stroking it, it was so silky and smooth.

Shelagh laughed. "What a strange question! From you, I mean."

"I've a reason for asking."

"I do it myself, mostly. But if there's something special I go to Charlotte Gray's. Why?"

So I told her what Tom Baines had said about Meg's employment.

Shelagh sat up straight. "Now look, darling," she said, "I'm just a little *bored* hearing about Tom Baines."

"It's Meg I want to find."

"Meg, too. You've an obsession about this, Mark. Leave it to those whose business it is."

"We wouldn't have got to know each other if I had. Anyway, I just wondered if you might have come across her—"

"Well, I haven't." She smiled. "Darling, we've been engaged less than two days. Let's talk about things that *matter*."

So we talked about the ring, and the wedding, and Gwen's party on Saturday.

"Guess who she's inviting," I said. "Tom Baines."

Shelagh laughed. She had a sense of humour, thank God.

When I went into the office after morning surgery on Friday, Edward Cohen was there. He didn't often stay for coffee, his time was too precious.

"Ah, Mark!" he said. "Just the man I wanted to see."

Mandy came in with my cup. She'd been very quiet the last day or two. Distant. Just like when I first came.

She said to me: "Mr. Peterson rang. He'd like you to call."

"Is it urgent?"

"No."

"All right. Thanks." She went out.

Edward Cohen regarded me through his thick glasses. "It's about Miss Armitage I wanted to speak." He was very formal, very correct. It had taken him a month to call me by my first name; and Mandy would always be Miss Armitage to him.

"What about her?" I said.

"She asked me for a reference today. She's applying for another position."

I wasn't surprised. Mandy had been a fool to stay so long. Everyone took advantage of her, especially her own family. She'd do far better to cut the umbilical cord.

And yet I'd miss her. Why? Well, she was a challenge. I enjoyed sparring with her, trying to fathom what was behind the façade.

Edward went on: "Frankly we don't pay her enough. And we'll *never* find anyone so good."

"I doubt if money enters into it, Edward."

"Well, at least we ought to try, we ought to make an offer. But John's so—well, he's a little parsimonious, wouldn't you say? Because it's his own daughter, I suppose."

Cohen wanted Ben Radford and me to join him in a deputation to John Armitage.

"You'd better leave me out," I said. "I'm only the assistant."

"I need your support. In these matters Ben's a broken reed."

"All right. But it won't do any good."

When Cohen had gone, I spoke to Mandy. "I hear you're leaving us," I said.

She flushed. "He shouldn't have told you. I haven't got the job yet."

"Would a rise in salary make any difference?"

"No."

"I didn't think it would. . . . I'll miss you, Mandy."

"Will you?" She had a brush in her hand and was absently poking it into her typewriter.

She looked so forlorn, standing there staring down at the desk, that I put my hand on her shoulder in an involuntary gesture of sympathy.

She wrenched away. "Don't *touch* me," she said, her eyes blazing. "You're my boss, or one of them. If you've any correspondence for me, go ahead, I'll take it. If not, would you kindly leave my office?"

"I'm sorry, Mandy," I said.

I turned away. At the door I looked back. She was still blindly brushing the type of her machine.

Well, why not? I thought. I'd nothing to lose. "Would you do something for me, Mandy?" She didn't look up or answer, so I blundered on. "I'd like you to go round the hairdressers in Chalford and—"

"What?"

I explained about Meg.

When I'd finished, she stared at me for a long time. Then she said: "No, I won't do it for *you*. Be very clear about that. But I'll do it for Terry's sake."

Harold Peterson said: "I've decided to have that op., Doctor."

"Good for you! I'll have a word with Farnleigh and . . ."

I'd get him into hospital tomorrow before he changed his mind. "Been bad recently?"

"No worse than usual. No, it's not that. I've been thinking, Doctor. About our Lesley. How she used to nark at me and call me a coward. And so I was." He sighed. "Do you think it's true the police are on to the man at last?"

The newspapers had been hinting at sensational developments. And Superintendent Egmont had said that "an arrest by the weekend was a distinct possibility."

"There must be something brewing," I said, trying to sound more confident than I felt.

Mandy intercepted me when I came back from the Petersons'. "I've found Meg," she said.

"Mandy, how marvellous!"

"You're on at Vine Street tonight?"

"Yes."

"I've arranged to meet her at the Greyhound at eight o'clock. Can you be there?"

"Well, actually, I did say I'd pick Shelagh up and—"

Her eyes behind the rimless glasses were steely. "Then you'd better cancel it, hadn't you?"

I rang Shelagh and cancelled our date. She wasn't pleased.

She would be about twenty-five, I estimated. Too plump for my taste, but Terry had always liked them well covered. Fair hair, blue eyes, nice, restful face.

She had a pleasant voice, too. Definitely not a girl from the wrong side of the tracks.

Mandy introduced us and I got them drinks.

I wasn't sure how to play this. Would she be embarrassed if I mentioned her association with Terry?

I needn't have worried: Mandy had prepared the ground.

Meg said: "I can see the resemblance. But you look more *organised* than your brother."

"He was pretty helpless, wasn't he?"

She smiled reminiscently. "That's what appealed to me, I guess. Sex and sympathy, that was my role."

"How did you meet him?" I asked.

"My mother was a patient. *You've* visited her, I believe. Mrs. Raynes, Woodside Crescent."

Heavens, I'd been in that house only last week! The woman had bronchitis, and there was a grandchild. The daughter was out working, I'd been told.

"Terry was quite frank with me. He told me he *had* a girl friend—that was you at that time, Mandy. What he wanted from me was—well . . ."

Mandy smiled. "What I was too prudish to give him."

"Well, yes. And I thought, why the hell not? Why should I live like a nun while Bill—that's my husband—was making it with that redhead he went off with? He was great fun, Terry, and always gentle with me. Not like Bill in that either."

"Why did you meet on the golf course?" I asked.

"It wasn't always there. Sometimes he came to my house when Mother was away. She quite often takes Brian—that's my son —to stay with her sister. But the golf course was handy, I had a key to that shed, you see—I found it among stuff Bill left behind. Labelled."

Mandy elucidated. "Meg's husband was a greenkeeper before he ran off."

"I suppose it was wrong, what Terry and I did. It didn't feel wrong. He really needed me, I think. Especially after you left him, Mandy."

"After he left *me,* you mean."

"Yes, well, this girl he got hooked to—Miss Carey—I don't think she understood him, she was too impatient—"

Mandy said: "Mark's engaged to Shelagh Carey now."

Meg put her hand to her mouth. "Oh, I'm sorry! I mean, I'm not saying anything against her, Terry was head over heels in love. It's just—"

"That's all right," I said. "He needed a lot of reassurance, that's what you meant?"

"Yes. He got so depressed at times."

"Did he talk about it? Did he say what was worrying him?"

"It was his job mostly—he didn't feel up to it. And sometimes he thought he wasn't good enough for Miss Carey, he ought to break it off. . . . But the last week or two I couldn't help at all. There was something he was scared to talk about. He stopped seeing me—I think he was afraid I'd worm it out of him."

"You rang him the night he died?"

"Yes. I hadn't seen him for a week and I was worried."

"What happened?"

Terry agreed to meet her at the usual place. He said he wouldn't be free till half-past twelve.

Meg was in the shed by twelve thirty-five. When Terry hadn't turned up by one o'clock, she decided he wasn't coming and started to walk home over the cliff path.

She hadn't gone far when Bess, the Labrador, came bounding up, sniffing and licking. So she stopped and waited for Terry.

She was a hundred yards short of the Devil's Shoulder. It was pitch dark.

"I heard something," Meg said. "Could have been a shout, could have been a gull screaming. It didn't really register at the time, it was only *afterwards*. . . ."

She waited for Terry, but he didn't appear. And then she heard running footsteps.

"It was weird," she said. "I mean, to *run* along the edge of the cliff in the dark! Madness!"

As the footsteps approached, she became frightened and turned off through the grass, back towards the hut. Bess was at her heels.

"There was a kind of sobbing as he passed. I was *petrified!*

I thought it was Terry and he'd gone off his head. Bess took off after him and I never saw the dog again."

"It *was* a man, was it?" I asked.

"God, it might have been a Barbary ape—it didn't sound human."

She'd crouched in terror, hardly daring to breathe. Presently she heard a car start up and move off.

"Was that *all* you heard?" Mandy asked.

"Not another sound. The car had no lights on, either. I tell you, it was *weird.*"

"Where was it parked?"

"Must have been in that hollow near the shed. It was so dark I didn't see it when I arrived, but it must have been there already. I'd have heard it if it had come while I was waiting in the shed."

So the murderer was there before twelve thirty-five, the ambush had already been set. . . .

Meg went home. There was nothing else she could do, she thought Terry had had a brain storm.

Next day came the news of his death. Her first thought was that he'd gone back up the cliff path and fallen over. But that wasn't sensible. He'd driven away, hadn't he? Besides, if he'd come by car, where had Bess appeared from?

"Why didn't you go to the police?" I asked.

"I didn't want it to come out about Terry and me. . . . Besides, they might have suspected *me.*"

She attended the inquest. And when it was all glibly wrapped up as an accident, she wondered again if she could be wrong, and decided she wasn't.

But she'd trapped herself. If she went to the police *now,* she'd be in deep trouble.

"I saw you at the inquest," she said to me. "Someone said you were his brother. I had to do *something,* so I wrote you that note. It kind of eased my conscience, though I knew I was just being a coward."

"You've told the police now, though?"

"Oh yes."

"How did they trace you?"

"Through Bill. They wondered about the key to the shed."

"What did they make of your story?"

She shrugged. "They were disappointed I hadn't seen the man, hadn't even seen the car, and couldn't describe the footsteps. It was just somebody *running*."

"And the sobbing?"

"Well, that was like nothing on earth. Sort of gasping, animal noises."

I drove her home with Mandy. She said as she was leaving: "Terry often spoke of you, Dr. Kendall. He thought there was nothing you couldn't do."

The remark depressed me. I'd let Terry down all along the line.

Afterwards in the car, I said to Mandy: "I'm sorry to have wasted your time. It didn't help—I should have known."

"Didn't it? You must have missed the point, then."

"What point?"

"Read your Sherlock Holmes. . . ."

She sounded depressed, too.

CHAPTER 5

Mandy went straight to her room when we got back.

It was nearly ten o'clock: too early for bed, too late to call on Shelagh. I decided to take the dog for a walk. Bess usually shared the drawing-room with Gwen after dinner. I went to fetch her.

She came lolloping over when I opened the door, wagging her tail hopefully. John Armitage was with Gwen, smoking a cigar and drinking whisky. It was almost unprecedented to find them together in the evening, unless they had friends in.

"Come in, Mark," Gwen said. "Get him a drink, John."

"No, thanks. I've just come to take Bess out—"

"Please! We want your advice, don't we, darling?"

"No need to involve Mark, my dear." He was wheezing.

"Nonsense. Sit down, Mark."

I sat down. John fetched a glass and poured me a whisky and soda.

"We've been discussing Celia," Gwen said. "Ben says she's *frightened* of something."

"Of what?"

"She won't even tell *Ben*. He thinks she knows something about the murders and is trying to suppress it, even from herself."

"My dear Gwen," her husband said, "Ben Radford was just sounding off as usual."

"Darling, he understands Celia a lot better than you do."

John made an impatient gesture. "You know my views. But do as you think best—I'll not interfere." He looked at his watch. "I've work to do. Good night, Gwen. Night, Mark." He went out.

Gwen was frowning. "He's just not interested in Celia. . . . I've had a premonition she's in danger, Mark, I can't sleep at night for worrying. And now *Ben's* warned me as well. . . . I want to send her away till all this is over. My sister in London would take her. But John says I'm being stupid, we mustn't interrupt her schooling. What do you think, Mark?"

I remembered Tom Baines's theory that Celia was likely to be the next victim. "If it would put your mind at rest," I said, "then by all means send her away."

She brightened. "I *knew* you'd give good advice. I'll ring Joyce in the morning."

I took Bess by the familiar route to the golf course. The scene of the murders had a fascination for me. Spots of rain were falling, but the sky ahead was clear and a half moon bathed the rolling fairways in a ghostly light.

I was thinking about Gwen and Celia. A dull child of clever parents tends to be a problem child. The parents expect too much and are aggrieved when performance falls short; and this causes complexes in the child.

But Gwen's attitude was even more disastrous. By shutting her eyes to what Celia was really like, by indulging her in everything, blaming any imperfections on her asthma, and blaming her husband for *that,* she had ruined what chance Celia had of coming to terms with life.

Of course, any normal father would have seen what was happening and made his presence felt. But John Armitage had opted out, he acted as if Celia were no concern of his. *Or* Mandy, for that matter—he had no pride or affection for her either. It was a wonder Mandy hadn't gone off the rails, too. . . .

Bess was happily trotting ahead up the path that Terry had followed two months before . . . to his death. In spite of myself my heart beat faster as I approached the shoulder, my muscles were tensed. But, of course, there was no one lying in wait.

So we went down the other side, Bess and I, and took the short cut over the grass where Meg had crouched as Terry's killer ran along the cliff edge.

It had been dark that night. Not like tonight, when any car parked in the hollow would have stood out.

Bess was at the door of the shed, her tail wagging, asking me to let her in. They were creatures of habit, dogs. It was two months since Terry last met Meg here, yet Bess remembered.

I thought about Meg's story, and Mandy's odd remark: "Read your Sherlock Holmes. . . ." What had she meant?

Then it dawned. The case of the barking dog. "But the dog *didn't* bark," Watson objected. "Precisely!" Holmes said.

Or something like that. It was years since I'd read Conan Doyle, and my recollection of the story was vague. But undoubtedly that's what Mandy was referring to.

According to Meg, Bess came down the cliff path first. She must have been running ahead of Terry, she must have passed whoever lay in wait at the Devil's Shoulder. Yet she didn't bark.

Well, that was possible. But later, when the killer ran down the path past where Meg was crouched, Bess went bounding after him. And still didn't growl or bark. That was *not* possible—not if it was a stranger.

Therefore it was not a stranger. Therefore it was someone from Tramore Avenue.

No, damn it, that was going too far. Bess was slow to accept people, but regular visitors to the house would be regarded as friends: Ben Radford certainly, probably Shelagh Carey, perhaps even Tom Baines.

So it was a damp squib: it eliminated none of the six suspects. Perhaps not, but it did confirm that the killer was someone in the Armitage circle. I wondered if the police had taken *that* point.

I could hear Shelagh say, "Leave it to them, darling, it's their business." Or Mandy: "It's arrogant to suppose you can beat the professionals at their own game."

They didn't understand. I owed it to Terry to find the killer: it was as simple as that.

As I walked home with Bess, I puzzled over Tom Baines's remarks about motive.

Was there a link between the girls who died? Or were they chosen at random? Perhaps the murderer simply roamed Chalford at night and attacked teen-age girls as the opportunity presented itself.

Yet if there was no selection, it was remarkable that all three were aged thirteen and from the same class in school; and even more remarkable that one of them—Lesley Peterson—was attacked *twice*.

But why these three girls in particular? And what did Baines mean when he said the fourth victim—if there should be one— must be Celia Armitage? She was quite different from the others, not even in the same form.

And then an apparently insignificant fact came back to me, something I'd heard quite by chance. It linked Celia to two of the others. What of the fourth? I didn't know; but I could ask. Tom Baines or Shelagh would know.

It still didn't make sense, certainly didn't provide a motive for murder. Or did it? There was one person who just *might* be driven to kill for that reason.

I called on Ben Radford after surgery on Saturday morning. It was his day off, and he was in sports clothes.

"You just caught me," he said. "I'm off in ten minutes." He didn't ask me in.

"A couple of quick questions, Ben. About Celia."

"What about her?"

"Gwen says you think she's in danger?"

"I didn't say *that*. I said she knew more than was good for her. I meant for her health. I've had to step up the drugs."

"What *does* she know, Ben?"

"It's something she saw the night Lesley Peterson died. She's put blinkers on so she won't remember; but underneath it's bothering her."

"Is that why she invented the man in the moustache?"

"That's my reading of it."

From inside a petulant voice called: "Ben, we're going to be late."

Ben gave me a rueful smile. "Come here a minute," he called. "It's Mark Kendall."

Tom Baines came to the door; he too was casually dressed. "Harley Street's slumming this morning," he greeted me.

"Harley Street's in luck," I said. "I want to ask you something as well, Tom."

"I'm shaking in my shoes. Fire away."

"What age was Pat Richards?"

"Thirteen."

"No, I mean what was her *exact* age? When was her birthday?"

Baines smiled. "So the light has dawned! June 20. That fits?" It fitted.

Ben said: "What the hell is all this?"

"A rash of coincidences, Ben. Though whether they *mean* anything. . . . Perhaps Harley Street has a theory."

Yes, I had a theory. I said: "Ben, where was Celia born?"

"Here in Chalford."

"In the hospital or at home?"

"It was before my time, Mark. But I know it was in the Bruntsfield. Gwen's talked about it *ad nauseam*." The Bruntsfield was the local maternity hospital.

I was still only half-believing my theory.

Anne Ridley wasn't at home. Her sister said she was playing hockey.

So I drove to the school playing fields, which were on a cramped site in the old town, overlooked by decaying buildings.

I parked outside and went in. Several hockey and soccer matches were still in progress. Anne was in one that was being watched by a scattering of spectators, mostly school children. She looked the youngest player on either side, but moved with the authority and grace of a natural athlete.

"Darling, what on earth are you doing here?" I hadn't seen Shelagh approach. "You haven't come to put off *another* date?"

"No, of course not." Shelagh was the last person I wanted to see right now.

"Well, what then?"

"I'd like a word with Anne Ridley."

She looked perplexed, as well she might. "Anne Ridley?" she repeated. Then: "You're not still playing the detective, are you? Well, really, Mark, this is getting beyond a joke."

"I never thought it was amusing, Shelagh."

The whistle blew for the end of the match, there was the exchange of civilities, then the teams started to come off.

Shelagh said curtly: "I'm helping with the teas. See you tonight." She turned away and walked smartly to the pavilion.

Just a *shade* possessive, I thought. Her manner had subtly changed since our engagement.

I intercepted Anne Ridley. "Oh hullo, Dr. Kendall," she said easily. "I didn't know you were a fan."

"I'm not. I wondered if I could talk to you."

"Now?"

"No, after you've changed."

"Sure. I'll not be long."

I moved across to a soccer match. Among the spectators were Celia Armitage and two younger girls, one of whom I recognised as Helen Potts.

Helen was squealing: "Stop it, Celia. You're *hurting*." She sounded only half in earnest.

Celia had Helen's arm behind her back and was twisting it. Her face was flushed, her eyes bright.

"That's enough, Celia," I said sharply.

She looked up, then stuck her tongue out at me. But she let Helen's arm go.

Anne came running out of the pavilion. "Sorry I took so long," she said as I joined her.

"You didn't. . . . You're none the worse of Guy Fawkes Night?"

"No, I'm fine. It was just a joke—Celia gets carried away sometimes." She glanced towards the football pitch, where Celia and the other two girls were now standing, watching the game with arms linked.

"I know you've told this story before, Anne. Many times, no doubt. But I'd like to hear it again: *exactly* what happened on the night Janice Allen was murdered."

"Well, we got down to the creek about—"

"No, sorry, start *before* that. Janice arrived separately, didn't she? How many people knew her bicycle was out of action?"

"Nobody. I mean, we didn't know ourselves, Lesley, Pat and I. She just got the puncture on her way home from school. We used to meet outside St. Saviour's Church. We waited our usual ten minutes and then when Jan hadn't turned up we decided she wasn't coming. Then she passed us in Miss Carey's car!"

"Anyone else at the beach you recognised?"

"When we arrived, Celia Armitage was having a roughhouse with Helen Potts." She glanced across at them again. "Jan was stupid enough to interfere, and she got a mouthful from Celia. 'I'll kill you!' she shouted, 'I'll kill the lot of you!' "

Anne stopped abruptly, put her hand to her mouth. "She didn't mean it, that's just the way Celia talks. . . ."

"Yes, all right. . . . And then?"

"Well, they went away. We had a swim and then we sunbathed. There were quite a lot of people down that night, but I didn't know any of them. Oh, except Celia's mother—she came down and asked if we'd seen Celia. She often used to go looking for her if she was out late."

"What was said?"

She repeated the conversation they'd had. "Jan didn't *mean* to be cheeky," she explained.

"And then?" I prompted.

"Mrs. Armitage went away. I heard her going off in her car. We talked for a bit, then we had another swim. It was quite late by this time and everybody else had gone home. When we came out of the water, it was turning chilly. So we got dressed and started cycling home, Pat and Lesley and I. The last I saw of Jan, she was standing at the edge of the road."

"You saw no one else about?"

"Well, your brother was walking down the golf course towards the stile. *We* could see him, but he'd be hidden from Jan till he reached the stile."

"But apart from my brother?"

"Dr. Armitage's car passed us."

"Was he alone?"

"I never noticed."

"What about earlier, when you were still on the beach? You didn't see anyone hanging around then?"

"No." But this time there was a slight hesitation.

I pressed her. "You're sure?"

"I didn't *see* anyone, but—" She laughed and said: "You'll think this terrible, Dr. Kendall, but that last swim we had—well, the beach was deserted and for a dare I went in starkers. I mean, who cares nowadays? I just wanted to shake the other three, they were all a bit square. Well, I was sorry I did it, because I had this funny prickly feeling at the back of my neck: somebody was *watching*. A peeping tom." She giggled. "Not *the* Peeping Tom —at least, I don't suppose so."

"Imagination?" I suggested.

"That's what Inspector Robens said. But I thought I saw some movement behind these big boulders."

The door of the pavilion opened and Shelagh called: "Anne, are you having tea with us or not?"

Anne smiled sweetly. "Just coming, Miss Carey." And to me: "This was my first game in the School XI. I'd better not blot my copybook. Was there anything else, Dr. Kendall?"

"No, thanks. You've been a great help. . . . By the way, when's your birthday, Anne?"

"Third of August."

She should be safe enough.

I called on the matron of Bruntsfield Hospital.

"How far back do your records go?" I asked her.

"Ten years," she said. "Since the date the new wing was built and the whole hospital reorganised."

"And before that? Are they all gone?"

"Oh no, they're still in a basement in the old wing. But frankly, Dr. Kendall, the filing system in those days was deplorable." She shook her head disapprovingly.

"All the same it's not *impossible* to consult them?"

"What did you have in mind?" she asked.

I told her.

"Is it important?"

"Yes."

"All right, I'll see what I can do. . . . I'll ring you when I have the answer.

Finally the police.

Detective Inspector Robens was off duty, they told me. They offered me someone else, but I declined.

In spite of our antagonism, I could talk to Robens, he would listen and he would understand.

So I went to his house.

He was digging in the garden on this dull, grey November day.

"You must be keen," I said.

"I hate it. But it passes the time. Come in."

He stuck his spade in the ground and led me round to the back door, where he removed his boots.

We went into the kitchen where a woman was bending over the cooker stirring something in a pan.

"Margot, this is Dr. Kendall," Robens said.

She turned round, a small, faded, grim-looking woman. "How do you do?" she said shortly, then to her husband: "Lunch is almost ready."

"Keep it hot for me, would you?" He was already lighting a cigarette.

She didn't answer.

Robens took me to the sitting-room. "Let's have it, then," he said, coughing as he pulled on a pair of slippers.

He heard me out without interruption. Then he said: "We should have spotted these dates."

"You knew all the rest?"

"Oh yes."

"Then why in God's name haven't you *acted?*"

"Made an arrest, you mean?"

"Yes."

"Not enough evidence. No motive for a start."

"*I've* suggested a motive."

"A crackpot one." He waved a hand to forestall my objection. "Oh, I accept it. But would a jury?"

"I don't see why not. No one has ever suggested the murderer is *sane.*"

He tossed an empty cigarette packet into a wastepaper basket. "I ought to cut down on these," he muttered.

"Yes, you ought."

He wasn't listening. He said: "We've proved it *could* only be one person. Reduced the possibles from fifty thousand to six, and then to two, and finally to one. All the others are eliminated, they couldn't possibly be guilty, we *know* that."

"Then what are you waiting for?"

"You can't convict a person on negative evidence, Dr. Kendall. The D.P.P. would never allow a case to be brought. You can't ask a jury to find that X did it simply by proving that Y and Z didn't."

"There are plenty of positive indications—"

"*Indications,* yes. Not proof."

"So meanwhile a murderer—someone *known* to be a murderer —goes free?"

"There will be no more murders, Doctor. Be assured of that."

"And how do you find your positive evidence?"

"Excuse me a minute." He went out, and I heard raised voices in the kitchen. When he came back, he was lighting another cigarette.

"We're trying an experiment tonight," he said. And told me what it was. "It just *might* work, don't you think?"

It was the first time he'd volunteered information. I wondered why.

"It's risky," I said. "The child's not well. Her mother's sending her away tomorrow."

"Celia's agreed to cooperate."

Yes, but not knowing of the trap.

"Does anyone else know?"

"Only her stepsister, and *she* won't talk. And we've warned Celia not to tell anyone."

He had more confidence in Celia's discretion than I had.

Robens said: "I hear there's a dinner party at Tramore Avenue tonight. . . ."

"Yes."

"It did just occur to me that we might make the experiment more realistic if . . ." And he explained.

So that was why he'd revealed the plan: he needed my coop-eration.

"All right," I said. "But what were you going to do if I hadn't happened to call this morning?"

"Used one of our own officers to impersonate the driver. But this way it'll be more realistic."

He had another bout of laboured coughing. When he'd re-covered, he said: "I never smoked till I was forty. Started when my daughter died."

"Mandy told me."

"Ah yes, Mandy. . . . She's quite a girl." He looked as if he wanted to say more, but didn't. "See you tonight, Doctor. And make sure your timing's right."

CHAPTER 6

When I called for Shelagh, she was still dressing, and I had to cool my heels in her sitting-room. She'd never kept me waiting before.

Eventually she came in and pirouetted round the floor to show off her new dress.

"Like it, darling? It's called a vest dress. I got it in Bayne's this afternoon."

"It's terrific. A bit way out for Chalford, though."

She laughed. "Don't be stuffy, darling. I'm tired of playing the schoolmarm."

Yes, but there was a happy medium. . . .

"I've looked at rings, too, Mark. Lauderdale's got three put aside for you to see."

"I thought we were going on Monday—" I'd intended to let the jeweller know my price range in advance.

"Oh, but we *are*. This was just a preliminary canter. You'll *swoon* when you hear the prices. . . . But, of course, we don't have to choose from these three."

Not much . . .

She came over and kissed me. "I'm so excited, Mark. I've never been so happy."

"Me too . . . We'd better go, darling."

She put on her fur jacket and we went out to the car.

On the way to Tramore Avenue Shelagh said: "Is Mandy going to be there tonight?"

"So far as I know. Why?"

"I'm *so* glad. I was afraid she might sulk. I've a terrific admiration for her, Mark, I want her to like me."

That was the way Shelagh always talked, she was no different this evening. Why did it suddenly sound so hollow?

It's impossible to be wholly objective about a person. You form an opinion and you judge every action and every word in the light of that opinion. Then a doubt appears and the whole edifice collapses. Your revised opinion may be as false as your first; the truth probably lies somewhere between. But the damage is irreparable.

I was thinking: Shelagh Carey is a goddamned bitch. How did I ever get tangled with her?

And I knew the answer to that too: I got tangled because Shelagh spun the web and I walked in.

Before dinner there was champagne. The three partners all made little speeches, but only Ben Radford managed to sound convincing. Edward Cohen was by nature dry, and John Armitage —well, he scarcely made the effort to be agreeable.

Before we went in to dinner, Gwen said: "Ben, I'm worried about Celia."

Her husband said: "For God's sake, not *now,* Gwen."

It could have been a recording of my very first evening at the Armitages'.

"I'd just like Ben to *see* her. She was terribly restless and fevered-looking. I had to put her to bed."

So Ben went upstairs. I wondered if Celia would tell him what was afoot.

But when he came back, he gave no sign. He said: "She'll do. She's had too much excitement lately. I'm glad you're getting her away tomorrow, Gwen."

"I'll not feel safe till she's gone. . . . Well, shall we go in? Mandy, perhaps you'd tell the kitchen."

"The kitchen" was the daily who stayed late to help on special occasions. Actually, most of the work for this kind of party was done by Mandy.

Although the food and wine were good, the party never came alive. It hadn't much chance, really. Edward Cohen and his wife have no small talk, Mandy was at her most monosyllabic, her father was preoccupied; and I was miserable.

Most of the running was made by Tom Baines, though sometimes he did more harm than good. As when he said: "Don't you have the sense of *déjà vu?* I'm thinking of that night in September when poor old Terry—"

Shelagh said, smiling: "Tom, this is an *engagement* party, remember?"

"Yes, but it's so *like* that other night. The very same people, except that Mark's here instead of his brother. And everyone sitting around with long faces."

Mandy went out to get the coffee.

"The phone should ring now," Baines continued. "Remember, Terry got a phone call?"

I said: "I assure you I've no intention of walking to the Devil's Shoulder."

"Darling," Gwen said, "aren't you going to offer liqueurs?"

"What? Oh yes, certainly." John took the orders.

As Mandy came back with the coffee, the telephone rang. Baines said: "Right on cue."

Mandy answered it. It was for me.

As I went out I closed the dining-room door—a precaution Terry had failed to take, to his cost.

I lifted the phone. It was the matron of Bruntsfield Hospital. "I've got the information you wanted, Dr. Kendall."

"Yes?"

"The Bruntsfield had no private rooms in these days, but there was a small semi-private ward with four beds. That's where they were."

"All four?"

"Yes. . . . Funny thing, Doctor: not long after you left this morning, someone from the C.I.D. was along asking the very same questions!"

"Really? Well, thanks for all your trouble, Matron."

When I went back in, Shelagh said: "Anything wrong, darling?"

"No. Why?"

"I thought you looked upset."

No, not upset. Just sad.

Mandy finished her coffee and stood up. "I must go," she said.

Gwen said: "It's early yet. I do think that *tonight*—"

"I'm sorry, Gwen. I've another engagement." She walked to the door. "Good night, everybody."

Shelagh said: "*So* nice of you to be here, Mandy. I do appreciate it."

Mandy regarded her coolly. "Do you, Shelagh?" She went out.

It was nine twenty-five. The schedule was going to be tight. I listened. And presently I heard a car drive off.

Tom Baines had steered the conversation back to Terry's death. Almost as if he were privy to the plot.

Gwen was riding her hobbyhorse. "It's *disgraceful*," she said, "that the killer's still at large. All these empty boasts about an arrest this weekend—"

Here was my cue. "The ides of March are not yet gone, Gwen," I said.

"What?"

"The weekend's not over yet. Perhaps this experiment tonight will work the oracle."

"What experiment?"

"The thing Celia's helping in."

"What on earth are you talking about?"

I pretended surprise. "But surely you know? That's why Celia went off with Mandy five minutes ago—"

Gwen had gone white. "Mark, I don't believe it! Went off *where?*"

"The police are reconstructing the Lesley Peterson murder. They believe Celia saw something that night that's been blotted out from her memory. And the idea is that seeing all set up again may jolt her into remembering."

Ben Radford said: "This is *monstrous!* As her doctor I forbid it. She's in a highly disturbed state." He was blustering as usual.

I said: "Ben, you do want the murderer found, don't you?"

He subsided as usual.

But Gwen wasn't mollified. "Why wasn't I consulted?" she demanded.

"I suppose they didn't want to upset you." They knew Gwen would never give her consent.

John Armitage said: "When does this performance take place?"

"Ten o'clock. The same time as it happened."

"Over my dead body!" said Gwen, starting towards the door. "Imagine subjecting a child of thirteen to that! I'm going straight down there to—"

"I'll take you," I said. "But only if you promise not to interfere."

"Interfere! When my own daughter's being used as a pawn—"

"Gwen, we must give this a chance."

They all looked hostile now, even Shelagh. The clock on the mantelpiece was on nine thirty-nine. I was sweating with anxiety, yet I couldn't move till I'd convinced them.

"There have been four deaths," I reminded them. "*Anything* is worth trying that might lead to the person responsible. All right, Celia may find this harrowing, but it won't *kill* her. She'll be better off than Janice or Lesley or Pat. Or my brother Terry. A lot better off."

No one argued any more.

John Armitage said: "What's your role in this charade?"

"Me? Oh, I'm the villain. I step out of the car as ten o'clock strikes."

Gwen said: "It's nearly a quarter to now."

"Yes, it's time we started."

They all wanted to come, except the Cohens and John Armitage. "I can't," John said. "I'm on call." He wouldn't have anyway. The rest of us got our coats and went outside.

I said: "My car's too big, really. They think it was a Mini. If I'd remembered in time, I'd have borrowed yours, Shelagh."

"Too late now," she said.

"Yes."

A pause, then Gwen said: "You'd better use mine, then."

"Do you mind? That's marvellous."

Ben took Tom Baines in his car. Gwen drove her own Mini, with Shelagh beside her and myself in the back. It was now nine forty-six.

The two women were united in their disapproval, it registered in the line of their backs, in every inflection of their voices. They might have been mother and daughter sitting there, Shelagh in her brown nylon fur jacket, Gwen in her favourite white one. They talked to each other and ignored me.

I didn't mind. I was keyed up and nervous. The timing had to be just right, and Gwen drove so *slowly.* . . .

"Right at the fork, Gwen," I said.

"But it's quicker by High Street."

"Robens told me to avoid High Street, just in case Celia spotted me."

She flashed her indicator and bore right, followed the leisurely curve of Woodstock Avenue, just failed to beat the lights at Woodstock Road.

As we waited, Shelagh said: "Try not to worry, Mrs. Armitage. I'm sure Celia will be all right."

"But she's so highly strung, this could set her back for *months*."

I said: "The *lights*, Gwen."

"I'm not blind." She crashed the gears as she moved off.

Two hundred yards along Woodstock Road was the junction with Piper Lane. Here at the corner, outside Francini's Fish Grill, Lesley Peterson and Anne Ridley had stood chatting until St. Saviour's clock struck ten and Lesley started running up the lane. . . .

There was no one there tonight. Gwen turned left into the dimly lit lane.

"What now?" she asked.

"Keep going slowly. You see the entrance to the warehouse? Well, stop opposite that, half on the pavement. That's it. Now put your lights off."

She pulled on the handbrake, switched off engine and lights.

I peered at my watch; I could only just make it out. It was nine fifty-two. The drive had taken six minutes, though it seemed an eternity.

Shelagh started to open her door.

"Don't get out, Shelagh!" I said.

"Why not?"

"Celia mustn't *see* any of us. I've warned Ben and Tom as well."

"Is she there now?" People kept moving across the High Street junction, but we couldn't make them out clearly.

"She shouldn't be. Robens plans to get her to the corner as ten is striking, so it'll be *exactly* the same as the other night."

"And what happens then?"

"I open the driver's door and get out—"

"But you're not *in* the driving seat."

"Gwen and I will change places in a minute."

Gwen said: "You're not in the *least* like the man Celia described."

"That's just the point. They've told Celia they've a suspect who answers to the description. If she claims to recognise me as the same man, it *proves* she made the story up."

"That doesn't make sense, Mark," Shelagh said. She sounded puzzled, suspicious even.

I was gazing out of the rear window back down towards Woodstock Road. Every few seconds I glanced at my watch.

Time seemed to be standing still.

Nine fifty-seven. "All right, Gwen," I said, "let's change over before Celia gets there."

PART V

MANDY ARMITAGE

CHAPTER I

Hugh Robens came to my office this morning. Surgery was over, the doctors were out on their rounds—all except Uncle Ben, who was having his weekend off.

"I've just been speaking to your sister," the inspector said.

"Celia? I thought she'd gone to the playing fields."

"She has, but I intercepted her and talked to her in my car. I wanted to catch her away from—" He had to stop for a spasm of coughing. "Mind if I smoke?"

"Carry on."

He lit a cigarette, then completed his sentence, "—away from her mother. We want her cooperation."

"In what?"

"A mock-up of the Lesley Peterson murder."

"When?"

"Tonight. We'll have a car sitting in Piper Lane where the car was parked that night. At ten o'clock precisely a girl will run up the lane from Woodstock Road, just as Lesley did, the car door will open and a man will get out. . . ."

"And Celia will be watching from High Street corner?"

"That's right."

"What do you hope to demonstrate?"

"That Celia couldn't have seen what she claims to have seen."

"But you know that already."

"The shock will perhaps make her face the truth."

It was feeble. I said: "You're holding out on me, Inspector."

He grinned. "Mandy, I'm telling you as much as I'm allowed to."

"Why tell me anything at all?"

"Because I need your help."

He wanted me to smuggle Celia out of the house tonight without her parents' knowledge.

"Has she agreed to go?"

"Oh yes!"

I looked at him questioningly and he grinned again. "She sees herself as a star witness at the trial. She really believes now in that man in the dark overcoat, and she's expecting to see him again tonight."

I said: "Unless the stakes are high, it's not right to use a child for this. Especially a mixed-up child like Celia."

"The stakes are high, Mandy."

I nodded. "All right, I'll do it. What time?"

"You'd better leave by half-past nine. Drive her to St. Saviour's Church. We'll take over from there."

"It won't be easy, but I'll manage it somehow. There's a dinner party at Tramore Avenue tonight. Celebrating Mark Kendall's engagement."

There must have been something in my tone, for he said: "Why don't you fight, Mandy? Pride's a luxury we can't afford."

If anyone else had said that, I'd have given him the frozen stare. All I said to Hugh Robens was: "I don't fight that kind of battle."

I must be transparent. I hoped no one else had been as observant as Inspector Robens.

It wasn't till the engagement was announced that I recognised I'd fallen for Mark Kendall. It had taken a long time to break down my prejudice.

The quality of his work made the first inroad: you can't despise a man so dedicated. The patients took to him at once: he radiated confidence.

Out of respect grew—gradually, reluctantly—liking. The apparent arrogance reflected the narrow, studious life he'd led. He hadn't had time to master how to be diplomatic: if he thought he knew better than someone else, he *said* so—and why not?

He wasn't the smug, patronising man I'd built a picture of when Terry used to show me the letters. He'd been fond enough of his brother to jeopardise his career in an attempt to track down his murderer. And, arrogant or not, I found it rather endearing that he was prepared to match himself against the whole might of the C.I.D. It made me feel protective.

He was, in truth, a vulnerable man. Especially vulnerable in his dealings with women. He'd had an unhappy affair in the States, but apart from that I believe he was wholly without experience.

Early on he made tentative advances in my direction. But I fended him off. I was Mandy Armitage, I wasn't ever again going to lay myself open to being hurt.

I like to think that Shelagh had to work harder to get him; but that's probably self-deception. She has terrific sex appeal, and exploits it.

There you are, I'm being bitchy again, I can't say a nice word about that girl. I just *know* that for all her charm and modesty and sympathy, she's interested in one person only and that's Shelagh Carey.

Maybe it doesn't matter, so long as people don't see through you. If Mark thinks she's wonderful, then as far as he's concerned she *is* wonderful. She's much less prickly than I am, nobody would ever have a *comfortable* life with me.

Anyway, she's achieved her goal, and this time there are no snags. Mark—unlike Terry—is all Shelagh could hope for, and more.

And all *I* could hope for, and more. I realise that when it's too late. Mark cares about people the way I do. And I love him.

Well, he'll never know. I'm getting out of Chalford. I should have gone years ago. They won't miss me here: Gwen and Celia don't like me. And Daddy?—he'll just feel resentful that he has to break in a new secretary *and* pay her a decent salary.

I haven't anyone, really. It's rather frightening: if I dropped dead right now, there's not anyone—not in the whole world—who'd really *care*. . . .

While Gwen was resting in the afternoon, I spoke to Celia. She was furious that I knew what was planned for tonight. She didn't want a chaperon, she wanted to sneak out alone.

"Well, you're not," I said. "Inspector Robens' orders."

"You can't *make* me go with you."

"I can stop you going at all. I can tell your mother."

She gave in sulkily. "What time do we leave, then?"

"I'll come up about nine-twenty. You'll need to be dressed and ready to go."

She looked fevered, and her eyes were puffy. I said: "Celia, do you really want to go through with this?"

"Of *course!* There's nothing to it." She was trying to convince herself.

I hoped Hugh Robens knew what he was doing.

I didn't see Celia again before the guests arrived. Gwen put her to bed and sent Uncle Ben up to give her the once-over. He didn't seem too worried.

As an engagement party it was a flop. It wasn't just me—nobody seemed in the mood, not even Mark. He was restless and edgy and kept glancing at his watch.

According to Mark, one of us here tonight was insane and a murderer. Which one? I tried to consider it objectively.

Not me, not Mark. Not Edward Cohen or his wife—they'd been away when Janice Allen was murdered.

Not Shelagh Carey. No proof this time, just instinct. Much as I disliked her, she was too level-headed and *normal* to be that kind of killer.

Tom Baines? *He* wasn't normal: his very nickname—Peeping Tom—suggested a motive. I've read somewhere that homos often have a thing about pubescent girls. And I was certain he was a homo: he used to sound *jealous* when Terry took me out.

Which made one wonder about his friendship with Uncle Ben. . . .

Uncle Ben was an empty vessel; his opinions carried no weight, his blustering deceived no one, unless you count Celia. How deeply this rankled was hard to tell. But the mass murderer is often motivated by the desire to avenge himself on a society that despises him—I've read that somewhere too.

I just couldn't be objective about Daddy and Gwen. It seemed disloyal even to consider them in the role of murderer. Though why I should feel *loyalty* to them I can't imagine.

Gwen was addressing me. "Didn't you hear me, Mandy? The *coffee,* please."

"Sorry, Gwen."

I went out to the kitchen where Mrs. Jackson was stacking dishes in the dishwasher.

"Was everything all right, Mandy?"

"Oh yes, lovely, thank you, Mrs. Jackson."

I picked up the coffee tray, but she was still hovering. "Celia's been down for a Coca-Cola," she said.

"Has she?"

"Yes. She didn't look *well,* Mandy. You know the way she goes—all flushed and wheezing."

"Thanks for telling me. I'll go up and see her presently." Trust Celia to draw attention to herself!

I'd just taken the coffee in when the telephone rang. I answered it.

It was the matron of Bruntsfield Hospital for Mark. About a *personal* matter, she said.

Mark carefully closed the door behind him before he took the call. Again I was conscious of tension in his manner. There was something in the wind tonight, something Hugh Robens had told me nothing about.

I sipped my coffee and Cointreau. Gwen had made Daddy produce liqueurs. He always has to be prodded, he's incredibly mean about little things.

At nine twenty-five I stood up and took my leave.

Gwen was *furious,* she thought I was deliberately insulting Shelagh and Mark. But Shelagh, as always, was *very* understanding.

Celia was waiting at the top of the stairs. "You said twenty past!" she whispered accusingly.

"There's lots of time."

I got a coat from my room, then she crept downstairs with me. She was in high spirits, revelling in the cloak and dagger escapade. But she was breathing noisily.

In the car she chattered non-stop. "I wonder if it's the same man," she said.

"Who?"

"This man they've caught. Will he be wearing the same overcoat, do you think?"

"How should I know?"

"I did see him, Mandy, I *know* I did."

"And you'd recognise him again?"

"Of course! And then you'll all be sorry you didn't believe me."

One thing for sure: if the man who emerged from the car tonight remotely fitted Celia's description, she'd "recognise" him. She had to.

When I pulled up outside St. Saviour's, a reception committee of about half-a-dozen was waiting. Among them were Chief Superintendent Egmont and other senior officers. Evidently this was no routine exercise.

Hugh Robens explained the drill to Celia. "We'll get you to Piper Lane"—he pointed up High street—"at exactly ten o'clock. A car will be parked in the lane just where you saw it that night. As the clock strikes the hour, the car door will open and a man will get out. We want to know if you recognise him."

Celia was dancing with excitement. "And if I do, will you arrest him?"

"We'll see."

"Will he have a gun? Do you think he might shoot?"

"He won't have a gun." The inspector turned to me. "No need for you to wait, Mandy."

Celia said. "Yes, go away, we don't need you."

"All right," I said. "Don't get too excited, Celia."

She made a face.

I drove up High Street as far as the Woodstock Avenue fork,

then worked round to the lower end of Piper Lane. I parked fifty yards beyond the intersection and walked back.

It was edging nine forty-five. As I passed Francini's, I saw Anne Ridley inside, flanked by two policemen and eating a fish supper. She didn't see me. I guessed she was going to do the running.

There were no cars in Piper Lane. And the only pedestrians were a young couple strolling down hand in hand. I waited until they turned the corner into Woodstock Road, then I ran up the lane and concealed myself in McKenzie's doorway.

Nothing happened for a few minutes, then a car turned in from Woodstock Road, crawled up the lane, and parked right opposite me, half on the pavement. It was a Mini. I couldn't see who was in it.

I'd lost count of time. I risked putting my hand out into the dim light of the lane to see my watch.

It was nine fifty-seven: three minutes to go. But just then I heard running footsteps and saw Anne Ridley dashing up the pavement from Woodstock Road. As she approached, the car door opened and a woman got out.

Then everything happened at once. From the High Street corner came a piercing scream: "Mummy, Mummy, *Mummy!*"

Gwen froze momentarily, but swung round as Mark Kendall got out of the car. She made a sudden lunge and I saw something glint as she struck at him.

He staggered and fell and she raised her arm to strike again. But I was already across the street and had grabbed her arm.

We stood there, panting, like wrestlers. Dimly I heard the sound of running feet; someone was screaming. Gwen had the strength of the insane, I couldn't hold on much longer.

Suddenly it was all over. A couple of policemen were holding Gwen, the knife clattered on the pavement. But the screaming continued: it was from someone in the car.

I knelt down beside Mark.

CHAPTER 2

After he'd been in hospital a week, Mark sent for me.

If it hadn't been for Celia, I'd already have shaken the dust of Chalford from my feet. I had a job lined up in York, I was just waiting until Celia was well enough to be left.

Oddly it was me she clung to, not Daddy, not even Uncle Ben. I sat in her room for hours on end while she sobbed and raged and screamed. I didn't do anything—just stroked her head and murmured platitudes I didn't believe in. It seemed to help.

Uncle Ben came twice a day. And always brought news of Mark. The knife had punctured his right lung, narrowly missing the heart. He was not in danger.

On the seventh day, Uncle Ben said to Celia: "You're better now, pet, aren't you?"

"I'm *not*." But her tone was peevish rather than hysterical. She was over the worst.

He said to me: "Mark wants you to visit him."

"I'm not going."

"Not even to say good-bye?"

I didn't want to: my face went hot with shame when I remembered the things I'd said as I bent over Mark in Piper Lane and thought he was dying.

Uncle Ben said: "It's not like you to run away, Mandy." That did it.

He was sitting up in bed, looking pale and thinner.

"I've waited a *week*," he said.

"I've had regular bulletins from Uncle Ben."

"That's no excuse, Mandy."

Surely he ought to know *why* I hadn't come!

"Well, I'm here now," I said. "How are you?"

"I'd be dead but for you."

"Don't be melodramatic."

"It's true."

"All right, let's leave it there, shall we?" I couldn't bear his gratitude.

He looked hurt.

I said: "Gwen's been certified unfit to plead. That'll mean Broadmoor, won't it?"

"Yes."

"You knew it was Gwen? I mean, that performance last Saturday—it was all a trap to catch Gwen?"

"Oh yes." He sounded bored.

But I had to keep him talking. "What put you on to her?"

"She was always a front runner. It had to be someone who knew Terry would be on the cliff path that night and, as you pointed out, it had to be someone the dog wouldn't bark at. Of the few possibles Gwen was the only one who satisfied all the other criteria as well."

"What criteria?"

"For a start, the knowledge that Janice Allen would be walking home alone from Abbot's Creek."

"It could have been a chance meeting."

"It could, but remember, these girls weren't *random* victims, they were carefully selected. It's much more likely the murderer lay in wait for Janice, *knowing* she would be alone. And of our possibles, only Gwen and Shelagh had that knowledge."

"So far as you know."

"Quite so. It wasn't conclusive—only a pointer. There was another pointer, a more subtle one, in the Lesley Peterson affair. Lesley was lured to the spot where Janice's body had been found and only Terry's providential arrival saved her. Yet she didn't report the incident. Why?"

"Her diary explains that: the driver of the car was someone she knew and trusted."

"It doesn't exactly say that. Look at it this way: if *any* man picked up a schoolgirl and drove her after dark along that lonely road to the scene of the first murder, could she *possibly* believe his intentions were innocent? He could hardly have taken the road by mistake—it's a sharp right-angled turn."

"I see what you mean. So?"

"However, if it was a *woman,* Lesley might give her the benefit of the doubt, for at that stage everyone assumed the killer was a man. So, what we deduce from the entry in the diary is simply that the driver was a woman. . . ."

"In other words, Gwen or Shelagh again, since it had to be someone from that dinner party?"

"Or you, Mandy. . . . But the betting was heavily on Gwen."

A nurse came in with tea. She frowned at Mark. "You mustn't tire yourself, Dr. Kendall."

It was my cue. "I'd better go," I said.

"No, please, Nurse. She's doing me good. Honestly. It's not like yesterday."

The nurse shrugged, smiled and went out.

"What happened yesterday?" I asked.

He didn't answer. He said: "When are you going to throw away these glasses?"

"Get on with your story."

"And let your hair loose, put make-up on, buy some exciting clothes—you'd be *terrific,* Mandy."

I flushed with anger. "Get on with your story," I repeated. Inexperience didn't excuse *that* gaffe.

He sighed. "Where were we? Oh yes, Lesley Peterson. Well, Terry didn't report the incident either—which wasn't surprising if you knew Terry. And clearly the murderer did know Terry." He sipped his tea. "For ten days Terry brooded, then decided, as usual, to pass the buck to me. Whereupon he was immediately dispatched. How did the killer *know* when to strike?"

I'd worked that out for myself. Terry's unfinished letter to his brother, found after his death, made it plain he was about to spill what he knew. Who could have seen that letter? Well, Gwen was in and out of his room every day. . . .

Mark continued: "Then Lesley herself was murdered. And again it implied knowledge possessed by very few—knowledge that she regularly went home from the cinema unescorted. Her own parents didn't know that. But Gwen knew: I heard Celia tell her."

"So Gwen lay in wait in Piper Lane?"

"Yes, and that's when her luck deserted her. Celia spotted her pulling Lesley into the car."

"Celia recognised her?"

"No, it was too dark. But she did see that it was a Mini and that the driver was a woman in a white jacket. And she knew her mother hated these girls. . . . The idea was so horrible that she shut her eyes to it and invented the man in the moustache and the dark overcoat. She was half-believing in him herself latterly and she certainly thought the police had been taken in. When the car door opened last Saturday, she expected to see a man like the one she'd described. Instead, it was a woman in a white jacket again and—well, you heard her reaction."

"That's what the police were wanting."

"Yes, they needed Celia's evidence."

The police had been satisfied for some time that Gwen Armitage must be the killer. True, there was no single incident for which she, and only she, could have been responsible. But only Gwen could have been responsible for them *all*.

She had no alibi for any of the incidents. Either she was out in her car or else (by her own account) at home in her room alone. Which by the law of averages was remarkable.

They couldn't charge her, lacking the kind of evidence that would convince the jury. No one had seen her in action and survived. Apart from Celia. . . .

There was the problem of motive, too. Sexual perversion? Possibly, but nothing in Gwen's past confirmed it.

Then Mark, prompted by Tom Baines, spotted something the police had missed: the three murdered girls—and Celia Armitage—were not merely born in the same year, their birthdays fell within a span of two days. And when Mark enquired further, he found the four mothers had shared a small ward in the maternity hospital.

It couldn't be coincidence.

"*There* was the motive," Mark said. "Jealousy. Insane jealousy. Gwen hated those other children who had turned out so much brighter and prettier than her daughter."

Yes, these mothers Gwen used to entertain when Celia was an infant—these must have been the ones she'd met in hospital. And the meetings stopped abruptly when it became clear Celia wasn't quite normal. . . .

It became an obsession. She did her best to mask Celia's deficiencies, tried, and failed, to have her accepted by her contemporaries. And the hatred in her heart grew more bitter with the years.

"When did she decide to kill them?" I asked.

"The idea must have been smouldering in her subconscious. But what sparked it off was meeting the girls on the beach that evening—all three of them, plus Anne Ridley. They weren't very polite about Celia, then Janice gave Gwen some cheek. That was enough to push her over the edge—that and the fact that Janice was going to walk home alone. Gwen drove off, but came back again and waited. After the others had gone, she offered Janice a lift. . . ."

"Why did she strip the bodies?"

"The final humiliation, perhaps. Or maybe just to confuse the trail. She was cunning. . . . And yet she made one thumping great gaffe. That was when Celia was telling her that Lesley Peterson was in the habit of walking home alone from the cinema. Gwen said: 'You'd think that once bitten, twice shy. . . .' That was clearly a reference to the incident in September when Lesley was lured to the golf course. I was so steeped in it myself that it never occurred to me to wonder how Gwen *knew* about it. But it niggled away at the back of my mind. If only I'd spotted it sooner. . . ."

It seemed to me he had little to reproach himself with. And he might have been killed for his pains.

I said: "That knife she produced—did she know she was walking into a trap?"

"She must have suspected it. But she had to go through with the performance just in case it was on the level. She even offered her own car. . . . But if it *was* a trap, she was determined I'd suffer for it. And by God, she was quick! If you hadn't—"

"This is where we came in, Mark."

"Don't be so prickly, Mandy. Am I not allowed to say 'Thank you'?"

"I just acted instinctively. Anyone would have done the same."

"Not *anyone*."

I wondered if he meant Shelagh, who had sat screaming in the car. . . .

He said: "Afterwards, when you were bending over me, do you remember saying—"

I stood up. "Good-bye, Mark."

"You said you loved me."

I was furious that he could humiliate me like this. "You must have dreamt it."

"I didn't dream it, Mandy. I've something to tell you."

"I don't want to hear." I was turning away.

"Shelagh and I have broken off our engagement."

That stopped me. "Why?"

"Because I don't love her—I never have."

"And she let you go?"

"Shelagh's not so bad. . . . No, don't look cynical, Mandy, it doesn't suit you. And neither do these damned glasses."

He was already untying the ribbon of my pony-tail.